A Dog Named Bella

Small Town Sparks #1

Bel Blackwood

To dearest Bella —
wishing you a very
HAPPY CHRISTMAS 2022
I know not the story so
if it's all wrong,
please forgive.
lots of love —
Mum + Jules
xxx ♡

Contents

Chapter One

Amy

ele

"You want me to interview a dead woman?"

"Stop playing around. She retired."

"Sure, that's what they say," Amy said. "But come on, you know what everyone's thinking." She leaned forward over her boss's desk, wiggling her eyebrows. "Who just walks away from an empire? I hope the budget for this assignment covers hiring a psychic."

Amy Kelly tapped a finger to the file that Savannah, her boss, had tossed across the desk to her. The top page was a simple dossier, but anyone who knew anything already knew the subject's details anyway.

Morgan Rachael Leithe. 34. Former genius CEO of Leithe Computing, brilliant philanthropist. Current whereabouts: unknown, following the fateful press conference three years ago when, without any warning, she'd announced her retirement from the public eye and vanished completely off of the radar.

"According to the internet, she died in a suspicious drone accident, and the woman giving the conference was actually a doppelganger hired to throw the cops off of the case. They have long conspiracy videos and everything. It's very convincing."

Savannah Whitney snorted. She may have looked like a graceful swan, but the head of Zero Nova Media was five foot nothing of spite and drive: terrible for working under, but as far as Amy could tell, perfect for running a media business. "Take this seriously," Savannah chided. "I've tracked her down and arranged an interview. We'll be the first press source she's talked to since her retirement. It'll cause waves—the sort of waves that we want to ride as far as we can." She reached over the desk and rested one perfectly manicured hand on the file. "Unless you want me to give this assignment to Georgie instead?"

Amy took the file as quickly as she could without actually snatching it out of the other woman's hands. "I'm seriously taking this seriously. I'm the most serious reporter on the planet. Seriously."

"Good," Savannah smirked, "because I've just given Georgie her own big project, so double-booking her would make things difficult. She'll be out on that new phone story for the next week, the same time as you."

That phone story was a big deal. Both of Savannah's rising star reporters out on big stories at the same time? Amy's stomach did a loop-de-loop. "So, Savannah... would you happen to be angling to hand out a promotion or two?"

"Oh, sweetie, no. You know that I don't give out rewards like that." Savannah shot her a bright smile.

Amy knew that perfect, charming, red-carpet-worthy smile inside out. When she'd first been hired, she'd practiced with a headshot of Savannah and a mirror, teaching herself how to look every inch the consummate professional.

Seeing that smile aimed at her own self didn't fill her with confidence.

"This is an opportunity for a promotion to senior reporter." Savannah held up a finger. "One opportunity. One senior role."

Between the two of us. Oh, shit. Amy squared her shoulders and tried not to let her face show her excitement. Cool, calm, collected, and cute, Ames. "And you're considering Georgie? Don't waste your time. I've done excellent work since I started. I got huge engagement on that planned obsolescence piece, and the numbers on my young entrepreneur bio series speak for themselves."

She put her hands on the desk and leaned forward—not standard behavior in a traditional office, but the sort of thing you got used to when you were working under Savannah, who liked her staff to have a little bit of sass and a lot of spine. "And I bring in the best bagels in the morning. I want this promotion, and I want it bad."

"Nice speech! I can tell you've been thinking about this." Savannah's eyes sparkled. "And that gets you in the race, but it doesn't mean you'll be the one crossing the finish line first. This isn't a school project. I don't give out ribbons to everyone for participation—or for bagels."

To her credit, Amy didn't roll her eyes. Savannah was only, what, a year or two older than her? 26, maybe, to Amy's 24? Being lectured like she was a dumb little kid by someone barely her senior made her want to wrinkle her nose.

Still, Savannah was the one that had built her magazine from the ground up, somehow, and Amy had to respect that hustle. "Yes, ma'am," she said. She picked up the file from the desk and tapped it against her forehead in a salute. "You want it, you've got it."

"That's what I like to hear," Savannah said, smiling her charming little fox-like smile. "You leave tomorrow."

"Where to? Is this a bikini kind of deal, or a snow boots kind of deal?"

"Oh, definitely the latter," Savannah said, and gestured towards the file.

Amy opened the manila folder. Clipped inside was a headshot of Morgan Leithe, cut from a professional bio. Even in a boring, everyday kind of business photo, she had presence. The woman was all high cheekbones and icy eyes, her mouth full but stern. A little bit Tilda Swinton, a little bit Xena, Warrior Princess.

Tucked behind the photo was a thick envelope branded Air New Zealand.

Morgan, you mysterious minx, Amy thought, touching the photo with a smile, here I come.

"Amy!"

"Georgie," Amy trilled back, stepping to the side to let her co-worker walk next to her. "Nice to see you up and walking! I was sure that that ass lift would have taken you out of commission for a whole month."

"Oh, Amy," Georgie sighed, gesturing toward Amy's body, "we both know that you don't know anything about getting work done."

She blew Amy a kiss, Amy flipped her the bird, and together they walked down the hallway and into the office. Keep your friends close and your enemies closer—at Zero Nova, those were often the same person.

Amy slid behind her desk, her brain buzzing with all the things she had to get in order ASAP, but something caught her eye. Or, rather, the lack of something did.

"Did Matias finally decide to get rid of his plants?" She frowned at the bare desk that was across from hers.

The copywriter's potted plants had been a bane of her office life. Sometimes a girl just wanted to do her job without spritzed water raising the humidity and making her hair curl, or sudden gnat infestations, or having to deal with a grown man happily singing hip-hop songs to his miniature succulents as he worked.

Georgie didn't look up from her phone. "He got kicked down to contract work. No decorations for hot-deskers!"

Amy winced. "Ouch."

"What, you didn't see his Facebook post?"

Had she? Amy was used to scrolling with her brain turned off. Yeah, yeah, someone's kid was always having a birthday, or someone was moving into a new house, or someone's dog was having a bar mitzvah... Amy had got into the habit of flicking past all of their important life events in the swipe of one bored thumb.

That... probably made her a terrible friend, didn't it? The idea that Georgie of all people was a better friend than she was was not a nice one. Amy had once watched the woman shout a barista into tears over the heinous crime of spelling her name with a Y.

"I bet it was the algorithm," she lied. "You know how it is."

Georgie slumped her dainty little chin into her hand. "Apparently he didn't get any warning." She sighed. "Well, at least we didn't have to sign a card. That's always sooo awkward."

"Don't be a dick." Matias had been a decent journalist, and, despite the plants, a decent desk neighbor. Never blasted terrible music on his headphones, never complained too much about his love life, and never ate fish in the lunchroom. What more could a fellow employee ask for? "This place is going to be a lot quieter now."

"I know, right?" Georgie screwed her mouth to the side. "First Julie in marketing, then Tom in editing. You know, tall Tom, the one that looked like a viking? And now poor weird Matias and his plants."

"Wait, Tom got canned, too?" Amy bit her lip.

It wasn't a complete surprise. She had noticed a certain amount of quietness spreading in the office. When she'd first started, the place had been a hive, full of bright-eyed (caffeinated) journalists (busybodies with keyboards) doing important work (emails, bagel runs, gossiping about who had slept with who).

Over the past few months, though, the thronging hive had dwindled. At first Amy hadn't noticed, but eventually the office space had gained a certain thinned-out appearance. No-one had to wage war for the desks closest to the windows anymore.

Anyone in the media world knew what that meant. The last senior reporter had just moved on to greener fields, landing a position in a more established company. Amy appreciated the fact that that left his position open (namely: for her to step into, no matter what Georgie thought), but...

She chewed her lip. "This doesn't look good, does it?"

"It doesn't look great, no. I thought this magazine was doing well, but..." Georgie shot her a look. "You were in Savannah's office for a while, weren't you? Everything peachy?"

"Hmm? Oh yeah, everything's peachy, I didn't get laid off." Amy stared down at her file like it was a strange artifact, then picked it up and gave it a little wave. "The opposite, actually. A big story. You have one too, right?"

"Oh, you are an actual reporter after all!" As Amy rolled her eyes, Georgie picked her own matching dossier up from her desk. "This? Just a little thing that will get me that senior reporter job."

"Nope, that promotion is allll mine. The only job waiting in your future is a do-over when your ass eventually deflates."

"Aww, she thinks that she's clever. I love that for you," Georgie said, and then looked at her phone as it started buzzing. "Okay, babe, I have to take this. Mwah."

"Go to hell," Amy trilled, returning the air kiss.

When the sound of Georgie's heels had faded away, Amy sat down at her desk and stared at the folder like it was some kind of venomous snake.

Five minutes ago, she'd been ready to scream her good news to the entire world. Now, though, Matias's empty desk had put a dampener on her mood. It was one thing to have a goal finally in reach, but it was another thing entirely to know that other people had fallen by the wayside —and that that same fate was waiting for her if she failed, too.

Perfect little trust-fund Georgie had a safety net to fall back on.

Amy had no-one.

She was going to have to be perfect. That was all.

But always being perfect had worked for her this far, hadn't it?

elle

By the end of the workday, Amy had managed to shake off the gloom of Matias's empty desk. When she went home, it was with a spring in her step and a head buzzing with ideas.

"Honey, I'm home!" she sang in her doorway, slipping out of her heels.

As always, her empty apartment gave no reply.

Humming off-tune, she put her shoes in the exact place she wanted, her bag in the exact place she wanted, and stripped naked as she walked through her apartment.

Some people thought that being alone meant being lonely. As far as Amy was concerned, those people just couldn't appreciate the pure joy of keeping your life exactly the way you wanted it. No significant other to leave clutter in their wake, or change the settings on your thermostat, or use up all the milk. Bliss!

She carefully hung and folded her work clothes, and then wriggled into some cozy yoga pants and an old tee.

It was time for The Planner.

Amy hadn't escaped from her tiny, terrible backwater hometown by simply wishing that one day someone rich and powerful would appear and whisk her away. Wishing on stars was for suckers. Jiminy Cricket may have been able to carry a tune, but he didn't have a clue about paying the rent.

Instead, as a teen, Amy had plotted a careful trajectory away from her unsupportive family and lack of career prospects, making an escape route by the use of one big master planner. It had changed form over the years, spanning across different notebooks and diaries and calendars, bursting with tacked-on post-it notes and scribbled addendums, but it was a constant part of her.

Everything in her life was accounted for, marked out decisively on the calendar. Smaller goals littered the pages, defining the carefully ordered future that was waiting for her: finding a more stylish apartment, a holiday to Europe, increasing her workout regimen, upskilling and moving on to bigger and better steps in her career, getting regular scheduled medical checks as recommended, beginning to look for a wife...

All that Amy had to do in order to have a happy life was to obey her planner.

It was simple. Easy. It left no room for doubt.

Back in the years when she'd been a scared and lonely teenager, being bullied in a hopeless homophobic little hole of a town, she could look at her calendar and put her faith in the timeline that spanned its neat little boxes. Its black-and-white rules had forced her to submit new written pieces for critique and competitions every week, and had her applying for scholarships and grants no matter how miserable she was, until her efforts had eventually paid off and launched her off into her new life as a tech journalist.

Opportunity for promotion, she thought, frowning as she flicked through her current book, and then tapped a finger to the page she was looking for. I wasn't expecting this for another four to six months! This puts me ahead of schedule. Yesss, go team Amy!

Her phone went off. Amy's stomach sank at the unexpected sound. Please don't be Savannah saying "I've changed my mind and given your assignment to Georgie, that incredibly fake personality and that even faker ass won me over after all, get ready to join Matias in freelance hot-desk hell..."

Instead, it was something nearly even worse: a text from a friend she hadn't caught up with in a while. i got my placement!! ames do you wanna come out and celebrate with me?, Olivia had typed. it's been waaaaaay too long, lol!

Amy slumped back against her couch, groaning out loud. Her mind danced with all the thoughts of all the things that a long flight entailed: picking outfits, packing her luggage, planning the trip... not to mention getting ready to interview a billionaire.

There was no way that she was going to try to wing all of that the next morning, hung over two hours before lift-off. She had to be on her A-game. This was important.

I can't, Olivia, she messaged back, I'm travelling for work tomorrow. Rain check?

The typing indicator flickered, and then Olivia's reply popped up. ur always so busy now tho... i haven't seen u in so long... maybe someone kidnapped u and is impersonating u to keep the act up...

We just went to that bar with the mechanical bull, right?

that was like six weeks ago

Amy frowned. Had it been that long? She looked down at her planner, turning the pages back and forth, but the new bright red entry for PLAN TRIP kept drawing her eyes back to it. I'm so busy with work these days. Sorry, Olivia, I'll make it up to you.

Amy watched the little '...' flicker on and off as Olivia typed. It went on for a long time, but when her next message appeared, it was just a simple ok.

Nope. Nuh-uh. Amy simply did not have the time to deal with whatever that meant—though it didn't take a genius to figure it out.

The thought of being Amy, A Terrible Friend was too depressing, so instead she put her phone down, got up, and went over to her home office desk. Whenever her personal life got complicated, it was always so much easier to be Amy, A Great Reporter instead.

She sat down in her chair and pulled up a search for her next target.

The screen filled with pictures of Morgan Leithe: Leithe giving a presentation on green energy, her glacier-blue eyes bright; Leithe shaking hands with shiny-eyed students, the ghost of a smile just barely visible at the crook of her mouth; Leithe handing out an award for tech innovations, looking every inch the sleek and slick professional billionaire that she was famous for being...

Every single photo would be out of date by now, Amy mused. What did Morgan Leithe look like these days? Was she tanned from lying around on exotic beaches, or had she locked herself up like a consumptive Victorian, wasting away until she was a skinny, pale ghost of a person? Happier or sadder? More down to earth, or more aloof? The same, or different? Secret clone hired to cover up a conspiracy, or the real deal?

Morgan Leithe, she thought. Why did you disappear?

Chapter Two

Amy

TODAY'S PLANNER (ORIGINAL VERSION):
9am: Touch down in Auckland airport. Collect your luggage. Grab some quick breakfast to go.

11am: Catch the transfer bus to the sleepy little ski town of Ohakune. Go over your plan for the interview during the ride.

1pm: Arrive in town, and check in to the B&B. Freshen your hot self up! Get ready for your first contact with Morgan. Be professional, be polite, be prepared.

You've got this!

TODAY'S PLANNER (AMENDED VERSION):
9am: Touch down in Auckland airport after eighteen hours of a kid kicking your seat. Discover that your luggage, searching for newfound independence and a spirit of adventure, has instead touched down in Sydney, Australia.

11am: After dealing with unhelpful customer service for an hour, sprint through downtown Auckland and just barely make it to the transfer bus. Stuff yourself into a long-haul bus seat which was apparently designed by the Spanish inquisition. Get out your plan for the interview. Promptly fall asleep.

1pm: Stumble off of the bus, and stagger into the B&B like a stinky jet-lagged zombie. Have a shower that feels so good that you want to cry.

Ask the front desk where you can buy a change of clothes, because you can't exactly interview one of the world's most powerful women in creased redeye clothes. Get pointed towards the only place to buy clothes that's open right now: the tourist gift shop.

You are now still a jet-lagged zombie, but, thanks to the fact that the local economy revolves around root vegetables, you are now a jet-lagged zombie in a sweater bearing a picture of a large cartoon carrot.

Maybe planning your first contact with Morgan can wait until after you find somewhere that does coffee. Like, a lot of coffee.

ele

Thankfully, the nearest source of coffee turned out to be easy to find. The Bellbird, a cute little cafe, was located directly opposite the B&B. In a stroke of coincidence, this was just about the extent of what Amy's brain cells could manage after the flight from hell.

As she'd gazed through the tiny window of the plane, New Zealand had unfolded underneath her in brilliant shades of emerald. Unfortunately, Amy had been able to see exactly zero of this as she'd run through the streets of Auckland to chase down her bus.

As she crossed the road, Amy took a moment to take in the scenery for the first time since touching down.

The air was crisp with a wintery bite, fresh and clear enough to make her lungs ache, and the snow-covered mountains on the horizon definitely let her know that she was no longer in a hot American summer. Small birds flitted in the boughs of the thick alpine trees that ran alongside the road, completely new to Amy. Their cheerful little songs piped up over the sound of creeks babbling, snowmelt streams running through the pines nearby.

This place was a gorgeous little slice of wilderness.

Amy couldn't wait to leave.

Where was the hustle and bustle? How was the Wi-Fi? Where was the nearest hot yoga gym? She shuddered. This place would look pretty on a postcard, but who would want to live in a postcard? No, thank you. Boring.

Shuddering, Amy pushed open the door of the Bellbird. Despite how quiet the streets were outside, the little cafe was full of locals. It had been a long time since Amy had stepped foot in a quiet rural town—and the last time she had been in one, she'd been desperate to leave to start her new life.

But despite being on the opposite side of the world, the vibe in the cozy little rustic cafe was just the same as the diner in the town she'd grown up in. The old folks eating their eggs and chatting about stories in the newspaper, the mom trying to get her toddler to eat his food instead of smearing it on his face, the grumpy-looking folks grabbing a cup of coffee by themselves over their lunch breaks... something about the sight made Amy feel a little soft inside.

"Nice jumper," the woman behind the counter said, pleasantly. "What can I get you?"

"A large coffee, please." Amy's stomach growled out a squiggly little sound, embarrassingly loud despite the background noise of the other patrons. "And, um, something to eat. Whatever you have that's hot and ready right now."

"How would a stack of hotcakes tickle your fancy?"

A day ago, Amy would have paused to consider the calories. At that moment, it was like an angel had descended from heaven right in front of her, bearing sugary treats. Instead of saying I have never wanted something more in my life, oh my god, you absolute savior, she settled for a simple "Yes, please."

She'd asked for something right now, and the proprietress—Marie, according to the grinning photo of her on the wall labeled with Ohakune's #1 coffee maker 2019!—delivered on that. Within the minute, she'd dished up a heaping pile of hotcakes, thick and piping hot and slathered in jam. Amy's mouth watered at the sight.

Instead of leaving Amy to unhinge her jaw and devour the hotcakes like a slavering wolf, though, Marie smiled and hung around. "So, what brings you into town? Here for the skiing?"

"Work, actually." Amy said as politely as she could from around a stuffed mouthful, and then rolled her eyes in bliss. "Oh my god, that's good."

Marie beamed with pride. "That's homemade jam, straight from local strawberries. My daughter, Kaia, makes it!" She gestured to the wall, where there was a framed photo: Marie and another, younger woman, the family resemblance strong between them despite the fact that Kaia had a mohawk, both pouring buckets of strawberries into pots, matching smiles on their faces.

Small towns, huh? Amy smiled despite herself. In the rushed pace of the city that she'd grown used to, people wanted their coffee with the minimum of human interaction possible. Usually, they didn't even get off of their phones when they were ordering. Getting the barista's whole life story? No thank you.

Still... "That's really cute," Amy said, and meant it.

"Aw, cheers, love. So, what line of work are you in?" Marie continued. "Not many people come around here for work unless it's up on the ski fields."

Before answering, Amy swallowed another mouthful of hotcake and jam. Finally, it seemed like the day was starting to take mercy on her. Okay, sure, she was a little behind on her planner's schedule, and she was more than a little jet lagged, and instead of Balenciaga she was wearing a baggy sweater with a picture of a happy carrot doing a little dance—but she was finally where she needed to be, she was fed and full of coffee, and she was ready to get to work.

"I'm a journalist, actually."

Marie's eyes shone. "Oh, that's exciting! Are you here to write about travel? We get those sometimes, too. It's a good time of the year for that."

"No, actually. I'm here to interview someone—a woman called Morgan Leithe."

Marie raised her eyebrows. "You mean...?" She gestured behind Amy.

Slowly, Amy turned her head.

At the table in the corner was a woman, one of the grumpy regulars that Amy hadn't given a second glance to when she'd walked in, too consumed by her desperate need for caffeine.

Tall. Pale. Intense cheekbones.

Oh.

She was staring straight at Amy, those unmistakable glacier eyes flaring with something indescribable. Despite the dowdy knitted sweater she was wearing and the way that her hair was poking out from under a woolen hat, it was clearly Morgan.

And she looked pissed.

"You're who's interviewing me?" she asked from across the room. Her sharp American accent instantly made her stand out against the rounded, soft sounds of the locals' accents.

The chatter in the room came to a halt. Everyone looked over at Amy.

Not the best start! Not the best start!!! "Uh, yes! That's me! Hi." Amy rushed to stand, hoping desperately that she didn't have jam on her, and held out her hand. "I'm Amy Kelly, I'm with Zero Nova Media—"

Morgan stood up from her chair, her icy glare pinning Amy in place. A wash of cold sweat ran over Amy's skin. "The interview's off."

Without so much as another word or a look back, she stalked out of the cafe.

The rest of the customers gave each other meaningful looks, and then shrugged and gave up the stifled silence to go back to their meals. Amy was left standing in the middle of the cafe, staring at the door, the sight of Morgan's retreating back burning into her retinas.

The interview's off.

Three little words had murdered Amy's future in cold blood.

"Cheer up," Marie said, giving Amy's shoulder a pat. "She's a bit of a prickly sort, hey?"

ele

TODAY'S PLANNER (ORIGINAL VERSION):

Wednesday: Initial interview. Then get back to your B&B base, get the bulk of the interview blocked out from your notes, and identify what else would really make this baby pop!

Thursday: Schmooze Morgan some more for those last little tidbits of information. Really make her come across on the page. Know your structure. Work your angles.

Friday: You should have everything that you need. Get down to brass tacks and start typing your little heart out. You've got this!

Saturday: You should be well and truly done by now, but Savannah doesn't need to know that. Maybe check out the ski fields in town before you leave for your flight home! You deserve a treat.

TODAY'S PLANNER (AMENDED VERSION) (AAAARGH) (I'M SCREWED):

Wednesday: Try to get in contact with Morgan. She's not answering her phone. She's not answering her emails.

Thursday: The contact situation has not improved. Desperately try to shake down locals for info. Discover that this is nearly impossible, because despite living in town for three years, Morgan keeps to herself and barely interacts with anyone. The woman might actually be a ghost.

Friday: The grand total of what you have for your world-shaking feature article: that on the rare occasion she eats at the cafe, Morgan likes her coffee black and prefers honey over jam. Is that enough for a high-profile story?

Saturday: Shit.

Chapter Three

Morgan

The reporter was still hanging around.

Being in self-imposed retirement and largely free of responsibilities, Morgan's days tended to blur together. When all you needed to do was to water your plants and walk your dogs, it didn't really matter if it was a weekday or a weekend.

Morgan Leithe had spent nearly two decades living her life to a strict schedule. These days, she took a perverse delight in ignoring her calendar and letting the days drift by.

Now, though, something—someone—was ruining that for her.

She let out a frustrated sigh. Around her, her dogs lifted their heads, curious about what their owner was stressing over.

Major and Boris, both pig-dog mixes, stretched out on the couch to get closer to her, their wet noses nuzzling at her just in case she needed comforting. She'd found the two of them at a shelter, on their last days after being repeatedly passed over. They looked too scary for the average prospective owner, the shelter staff had said. Pssh. Although they were tall and broad, the only scary thing about them was the stinging slaps that their happily-wagging tails could deliver.

Muffin, a scrappy little terrier mix, and O.J., a staffy, looked up from their beds down near the fireplace, ready and willing to leap into her lap with a comforting lick to the face if she needed it. With a cup of tea in hand, and no wish to have it sent flying, she raised a hand in the signal that let them know they should stay where they were for now.

But on the armchair across the room, Bella the Maltese opened one eye, assessed the situation, and immediately closed it again. She let out a long-suffering sigh, as if to say your emotional problems are none of my business, human.

Thanks, Bella, Morgan thought. She dispensed pats to Boris and Major to settle them back down. When nothing else happened, they went back to their favorite pastime: sleeping in one giant, snoring, doggy pile.

And Morgan was left with her new pastime, albeit one that was much less comforting: watching the reporter through her window.

It had been a few days since the reporter had shown up in town. Peeking through a gap in her curtains, Morgan watched from a distance as the woman made her way down the street once again, moving from the town's bed and breakfast to the cafe. It was no doubt the location from where all of the increasingly frantic emails that were appearing in Morgan's inbox originated.

From the way that the reporter slouched down the street, she seemed stressed out.

Well, tough. Morgan let the curtain fall shut again, and then let out a sigh.

She'd been expecting Zero Nova Media's CEO to visit her in person.

Instead she'd found herself staring down some sweet young thing, all charming smiles and big dark eyes.

Once upon a time, Morgan wouldn't have blinked at being paired with an attractive woman. Now, though, just the sight of the reporter felt like a slap in the face.

A few minutes later, on cue for the reporter's depressed walk to have reached the Bellbird, Morgan's phone started vibrating on silent once again. She glared at it until it stopped.

The sensible thing to do, she knew, would have been to call the CEO of Zero Nova Media and to tell her herself that the deal was off, and that she needed to call back her attack dog. Morgan now had no interest in doing Savannah's interview—not that she'd wanted to do it in the first place.

The reporter had been stomping around for days, now, no doubt stirring up the inhabitants of the small town that Morgan had taken refuge in. All Morgan had wanted in her new life in Ohakune was to live quietly, and despite three blessed years of snow and solitude, that was now apparently coming to an end.

Enough damage had been done, but if she didn't get the woman to leave, who knew how much longer she was going to stick around, asking questions to everyone in town? Morgan was already enough of an outsider—now the stares and whispers were going to be even worse.

Morgan picked up her phone and scrolled through her contacts. She hadn't touched them in a long time, but there was Savannah's name, still in her phone. Her thumb hovered over the contact.

Not too long ago, it would have been easy to make the call. Morgan had effortlessly mingled with some of the most powerful movers and shakers in technology and politics, handling multibillion-dollar deals with the deft savviness that had sent Leithe Computing on the meteoric rise to the height of its fame.

Back then, making a call to the CEO of some insignificant little tech magazine would have been entirely beneath notice. She wouldn't have thought twice about it.

Now, though...

Her thumb hovered, and then pressed down on the lock button.

You coward, she thought bitterly to herself.

Morgan's dogs watched as she put her phone down again, waiting to see what their master was doing. When it started ringing again, they watched as she stayed stubbornly staring at the book she was reading, and didn't give it a second glance.

"It's nothing," she said, to her audience. "Go back to sleep."

Chapter Four

Amy

TODAY'S PLANNER:
  10am: Check out of the B&B.
  1pm: Catch the bus back to Auckland.
  8pm: Catch the plane back to New York.
  Next day: Get murdered by a 5'0" hellion.
  Maybe kneel down to make it easier for her?

The days had passed like turns of the rack.

Amy was screwed. She was beyond screwed—she was doomed. As soon as she slunk back into the office empty-handed with her tail between her legs, Savannah was going to skin her alive and fashion her pelt into some sort of stylish statement piece, and no-one would miss her.

Marie put a plate of toast down on the table in front of Amy as she sat, her face dropped down on the table. "Chin up," she soothed. "It's not all that bad."

Visions of a life spent as haute couture danced before Amy's eyes. "It is," she groaned, too miserable to even nibble her toast. "This was my biggest big shot yet... and I blew it."

For some reason, Savannah had given Amy's schedule plenty of room to breathe: this assignment didn't call for hopping off of one plane, getting an interview, and then sprinting for the plane home, like some of her first assignments had.

At first, Amy had thought it was a rare treat from her boss. Now, though, it just looked like rope to hang herself with.

All this time, and she'd managed to get nothing.

Over the last few days, the plight of the sad American journalist had attracted the attention of the locals—or, at least, the ones that didn't have anything better to do with their time. Right now, a trio of backpackers made sympathetic noises at her. They sat around a bucket, watching as it filled from an intermittent drip from the ceiling. Apparently this task needed three grown people to supervise it.

"You could always just stay here," Will suggested, in the accent that Amy was just beginning to be able to recognize as Australian, close but strangely different to the local New Zealanders' accents. Natalie and James nodded alongside him, their dreadlocks bouncing.

"I can't," she groaned. "It's my last day. I'm already checked out of the bed and breakfast, and my bus leaves in a couple of hours. I'm out of time."

"No, I mean, like, just quit your job and stay here? We all did," Will said with his usual spacey grin.

"You all live your lives out of your rucksacks," Amy pointed out. "I don't think I'm cut out for that kind of life, guys."

"Hey, don't knock it," James said. "If you ever change your mind, I can get you a gig picking fruit whenever you want. Promise."

"Listen to James," Natalie said, wisely. "There are worse things in life that can happen, after all."

There were. Above Amy, the ceiling sprung a new leak.

Marie rushed over with another bucket, and shooed a now-damp Amy out of the way. "Bloody roof!" she swore, and then gathered herself. "Well, I didn't mean any of their garbage," Marie stuck her tongue out at the backpackers. "I just meant that maybe that woman will get back to your emails soon. I don't check mine every day, after all. Why not check again?"

Amy fought the urge to point out that there was a difference between a once-powerful leader of a tech empire, and an older woman whose only use for the internet was looking up recipes and sudokus.

She opened her phone. There was no reply to her many frantic emails.

Morgan, it's Amy, please get in contact with me ASAP.

Morgan, this is Amy again, I really need to talk to you about the interview that we have scheduled.

Morgan, this is Amy yet again; if you aren't going to give me an interview, could you at least kill me here and now, so I don't need to bother Savannah with getting her hands dirty? Thanks.

Okay, she hadn't sent that last one. But between the phone calls (many), and the emails (even more), and asking after every person in town that might have had the smallest contact with Morgan (a surprisingly small list), she'd tried every other attempt to contact Morgan that she could think of... short of hiring a squad of goons to kidnap her and tie her up with a microphone in front of her, that was.

That scenario was becoming more and more appealing by the minute, though. Amy imagined herself putting the finishing knot on a trussed-up Morgan, and leaning in to press a finger underneath her chin, tilting her face up to look down at those blazing glacier-blue eyes, saying now, are you finally going to talk, or do I have to get it out of you...?

Amy shook her head, clearing that particular scenario away. Ahem. She screwed her mouth up, chewing on the inside of her cheek. "Does anyone know her address?" she asked, not for the first time.

Marie sighed and looked at her hands. "Look, Amy, love, it's not that I don't want to help you, but..."

"But no-one wants to rat out a neighbor's personal info to a nosy journalist. I understand."

Marie gave her a relieved smile, openly glad that Amy wasn't taking it personally. "This is a small town. Some things just aren't done."

Amy wasn't going to try to put the thumbscrews to her. It may have been entertaining to think about tying up Morgan, but she knew a brick wall when she saw one.

Pushing the matter would just get her kicked out of the cafe. She was already about to leave in shame. Until then, there was no use pissing off the person who was bringing her coffee.

"Can I get a refill, please? And, you know, I heard that cyanide's supposed to taste like almonds, right? If you have any lying around, could you just slip it in with my almond milk? Thanks."

Marie snorted in amusement at Amy's dramatic American antics, and turned to head back to the coffee machine. When she'd left, the backpackers shared a glance. One by one, they began to get to their feet, stretching.

"Smoko," James said; by now, Amy had learned that this was Australian for I'm bored, time to drop everything and go outside for a cigarette. By the confident way that the backpackers used it, Amy was beginning to understand that it was a nearly religious term for Australians.

Natalie nudged Amy. "You want some fresh air? Come outside with us."

She slumped over the table, her eyes fixed on her phone. "No, I'm okay, thanks."

"Are you sure?" Natalie nudged her again, harder this time. "Fresh," nudge, "air," nudge, "is good for you." Nudge, nudge, nudge.

Her choices were apparently either to go with them, or be slowly and gently battered to death, ribs first. "Um, sure." Amy reluctantly got to her feet, and followed the trio outside.

The air outside the cafe was bitingly cold. To make up for her lost luggage, Amy had had to buy a few more clothes, all still from the visitor center gift shop—apparently the locals all shopped in the next town over, and Amy didn't dare leave and risk missing out on the chance that the stars might align and Morgan might change her mind.

At that moment, she was wearing a sweater featuring a potato wearing sunglasses. With its fleecy warmth currently defending her from the cold, she loved it more than she'd ever loved any designer piece. She shivered and huddled into its warmth, her arms crossed over the potato as if she was cradling it tight.

"Look," Will said, "I'm not gonna narc out a local to a journo, buuut..."

Amy's heart skipped a beat. She looked up from her potato. "But?"

"Well," Will looked sheepish, and the other two giggled. "Uh, maybe there's a house on the other side of town... and maybe the owner really likes cactuses..."

Natalie took a drag from her cigarette and exhaled a plume of smoke. "And maybe one time a stoned dickhead accidentally tripped over some of the pots in her garden and shit, and maybe that dickhead had to have the owner of that house tweezed a giant stinger out of his dumb face."

"Prick," James chimed in. When Will glared at him, he raised his hands. "I mean the stinger thing! I think when they're on plants they're called pricks."

"Anyway," Will continued, as the other two sniggered, "there's a house, and there's a lady who lives there who told me about how much she likes cactuses—"

"She was trying to distract him from crying," Natalie chipped in.

"Christ, I was so high. The point is... Stop laughing, you arseholes! The point is that maybe you should take a cactus to that one specific address I'm about to give you. Maybe that'd get you in the door?"

Amy raised an eyebrow, her heart racing. She'd worked with less before. But, still: "Where would I get a cactus from in—" She checked her phone. The clock was slowly ticking towards the departure time for the bus. "In the next two hours?"

"There's a few in the share house yard that no-one will miss. And, like, barter is the backbone of any solid community..." Will proclaimed. "So, like... do you have any sweet celeb gossip?"

ele

Amy certainly did. A few juicy tidbits about secret affairs and trips to rehab later, Amy was on her way.

Ohakune was small, a few main streets in a simple grid. It wasn't hard to follow the backpacker trio's directions to Morgan's house, even if they did include instructions like go left at Bob's place.

The promise of ice was in the air, the sharp cold stinging Amy's ears, and in the distance, a snow-capped mountain range loomed over the town, foreboding and grey. Amy remembered seeing it mentioned on the town's Wikipedia page—it had played the role of Mount Doom in the Lord of the Rings movies.

If it had been any other time, Amy would have taken a moment to admire the view. Right now, though, she was a woman on a mission, ready to march into dangerous territory. You and me, Frodo, she thought as she jogged along the street, a sacrificial cactus offering held securely in the crook of her arm. We can do this.

And then she was there, standing in front of her own personal Mount Doom.

Amy wasn't sure what sort of house she'd been expecting a runaway billionaire to live in, but it wasn't the slightly dumpy little cottage that she soon found herself in front of. It looked well-lived-in, like an old sweater; clearly someone had been doing little spots of work on it here and there, repainting a railing here and repairing an awning there.

There was a small leadlight bird in the corner of one window, clumsily made. To Amy's eyes, it was inexplicably charming, even if it did look just a liiittle bit like a marshmallow with a face.

Now at the mouth of the belly of the beast, Amy checked her watch. There was an hour before her transfer bus came to whisk her back to Auckland, and then off back home. If this last-minute gambit didn't work, she planned to spend that entire time crying.

Summoning all the courage that she could muster, she knocked.

Dogs barked somewhere inside the house, but no-one answered the door.

Was Morgan out? Amy chewed the inside of her cheek, thinking. But then, in amongst all the barks and yips, there was the faintest sound of a footstep creaking on a floorboard.

Gotcha! "Morgan, it's Amy from Zero Nova Media. Could I speak to you, please?"

Nothing.

A change of approach was needed. "Morgan, I'm not sure what I did to offend you, but you have my deepest apologies." Had Amy stolen the last hotcake in the cafe? Was the woman terminally afraid of vegetable sweaters? Did Morgan's star charts tell her to beware of Aries on Wednesdays? Amy had no clue, but whatever it was, she was ready to grovel in the mud if that meant getting things moving again.

Nothing.

Amy played her last card. Here goes nothing. "I bought you a cactus?"

There was silence—and then the door opened a crack. It was just a small gap, but it was enough to make Amy's heart race with anticipation.

A totem pole of small furry faces peeked around the open door to stare at her. An unexpected amount of dogs, all different shapes and sizes, looked up at her, their tongues lolling as their pointy snouts jostled for position.

At the bottom was a scrappy little terrier, the sort that was born looking like a ninety-year-old fisherman. Then above it was what looked like a wide little pitbull, all giant happy grin and eagerly tip-tapping paws, and then above that were two much larger dogs, looking friendly at the moment but also like the sort you didn't want to meet in a dark alley...

...And then at the top, of this clown car of canines, was, finally, the cold, icy stare of Morgan.

Has anyone ever told you that you look like Mount Doom? Amy had to bite back the urge to ask.

"What," Morgan said. It wasn't a question.

Amy held Morgan's stare for a moment, and then thrust out the pot that was in her hands. "I, um. Bought you a cactus. As an apology."

An apology for what, she had no idea. It seemed like a good tactic to take, though. At that moment, Amy would have happily apologized for everything up to and including nuclear warfare and single-handedly causing climate change.

"What makes you think I want that?"

"I have my sources," Amy said with a smile, exuding a confidence that she absolutely didn't feel.

If looks could kill, Morgan's glare would have annihilated Amy to ashes on the spot. Still, though, she wasn't shutting the door.

"I expected Savannah."

Of all the objections for Morgan to have—I've changed my mind about being interviewed; your cactus is inadequate; this is all a fever dream you're having after having too many overpriced airline sandwiches—Amy hadn't been prepared for that one.

"Sorry, we must have got a wire crossed somewhere... I'm Amy Kelly, I work for Savannah."

She stuck out her free hand. Morgan ignored it, her eyes focused on Amy's face.

Amy knew that women couldn't make it in the boy's club of tech without growing a thick skin and keeping all your emotions kept firmly under control... but just for a moment, Amy thought that she could see a flicker of uncertainty on Morgan's face, there for just an instant and then vanishing. "Savannah sent you to do this?"

"Yep. I'm here to let you tell your side of the story."

There was another long, icy silence, Morgan's gaze piercing as she searched Amy's face for something that Amy couldn't understand.

What was going on? Amy felt a blush beginning to heat her face. God of cactuses, if you exist out there somewhere, please have mercy on this poor journalist...

Whether Morgan finally found the thing she was searching for in Amy's expression, or if the god of cactuses worked his spiny magic, Amy didn't know. Either way, instead of shutting the door in Amy's face, Morgan let out a sharp whistle. The array of dogs disappeared from view, shuffling backwards.

The door finally swung open, revealing Morgan in all her glory.

At the Bellbird, Amy had been too caught off guard to really pay close attention to the other woman. Now, though, as they stared at each other across the threshold in one long silent moment, all that Amy could do was to stare openly at her.

She was gorgeous. It had been easy enough to dismiss that quality in Morgan's corporate headshot—pfft, who wouldn't look drop-dead stunning with a team of professional hair and makeup people at their disposal?

Here, though, Morgan wore nothing but comfortable winter clothes, her short hair finger-brushed away from her face, more shaggy than chic. A few wispy locks fell out of place to frame her cold blue eyes. There was dog hair on her pants, and a paint stain on one cuff.

And she was still gorgeous. It was unfair.

Amy looked downward. Morgan was wearing fluffy winter socks.

When she looked back up, Morgan was staring at her, one eyebrow raised archly. This totally did not improve Amy's whole blush situation.

"Well, are you coming in or not?" Morgan said. She gestured down the hallway, past the audience of patiently waiting dogs.

"Yes, ma'am!" Amy managed, and threw herself in through the doorway before Morgan could possibly change her mind.

Amy's gaze roved hungrily over her surroundings as Morgan led her through the house. Already, the machine of her mind was chopping up these images into a rough draft of text and pull-quotes: despite setting some of the longest-lasting trends in sleek, minimalistic design, Morgan's second life has found her in the midst of chunky knits and rag-tag rugs, settling down with mismatched mugs and shaggy dogs. More commonly associated with futurism than fur, the tech queen seems incongruous against the aggressively hygge backdrop, as she steps into a converted sunroom, populated with a raucous collection of succulents, clearly brought inside to weather the cold New Zealand winter. Then she turns and says...

"Do you want a hot cocoa?" Morgan said. Her voice was so flat that it was barely a question, but after the last few days of radio silence, it was still progress.

What was the correct answer here? If Amy chose poorly, would she be ejected out into the winter chill? Amy summed up her courage and gambled. "Yes, thank you."

Morgan nodded sharply, like a military officer receiving orders to carry out an execution, and stormed off into the kitchen. It was a very polite storm, but a storm nonetheless.

Adrift in the midst of dozens of mismatched succulents and inexplicable hostility, and being thoroughly examined by a pack of dogs, Amy felt a little out of place. She put the cactus down in amongst its peers, shuffling its pot around on the rickety paint-splattered bench until it looked juuust right. Thanks for the assist, little buddy! May aphids never bother you.

Morgan returned with two steaming mugs of hot chocolate in her hands. She passed one over to Amy. On it was a cartoon of a dancing potato.

"Ah-ha!" Amy exclaimed. "We match!" When Morgan stared at her, she shook her head. "Uh, never mind."

Lips pursed and keeping any comments on random potato outbursts to herself, Morgan sat down in an overstuffed armchair, and gestured towards the couch across from it. When Amy sat, the swarm of dogs rushed over to investigate her. It was a very polite rush—clearly Morgan ran a tight ship when it came to dog training—but under the combined curiosity of that many muzzles, anyone would have felt a little bit overwhelmed.

Morgan looked curiously at Amy, currently trying to politely avoid the wet noses that were investigating her pockets for treats. "You don't like dogs?"

"Oh, well..." Amy paused as a strange hesitancy crept up on her. "I grew up with them and all, I don't hate them. It's just... they're so messy and needy, you know? I like my life to be organized."

Morgan's only response to that was to silently quirk an eyebrow. For some reason, with Morgan sitting warm and comfortable across from Amy, in the center of her own clearly cozy little world, the words felt... immature. Childish. Amy shifted a little, fighting the urge to fidget.

You're a grown woman! A professional! Don't let her rattle you!

"Okay, let's get down to it," Morgan said, freeing Amy from her uncomfortable silence.

"Sure, that works for me." Amy got out her notebook and pen, and then set her phone to record, placing it down on the coffee table between them.

"The recording's on. Try to relax, and feel free to speak naturally." She cleared her throat. "I'll start with the big question, the one that everyone wants to know. Morgan, why did you leave?"

Morgan leaned back in her seat, her eyes fixed on Amy. Despite the comfiness of her armchair, she looked like a queen on her throne, about to hand out a life or death judgment.

"I was betrayed."

Chapter Five

Amy

Wait, what?

Amy's heart thumped. Before she could ask any follow-up questions to that bombshell, though, Morgan continued. Her voice was deceptively casual as she asked, "But I suppose I'm not meant to talk about that, right?"

"What do you mean?"

Morgan paused. Without taking her eyes off of Amy, she cocked her head to the side. "What have you been told to write?"

"Whatever you want to say?" Her heart racing, Amy rifled through the outline of the brief that she'd copied out in her notebook, as if any new information might suddenly appear on its pages to help her out. "Uh, around three pages, as agreed. Where you went, what you're planning next, that sort of thing."

Morgan reclined in her armchair, her steely gaze fixed on Amy. Despite the cozy surroundings, Amy began to feel like a suspect in a police procedural, sweating in handcuffs with a lamp shining in her face.

In any other circumstance, the idea of Morgan putting her in cuffs would have been something else entirely. Right now, though, Amy felt the thread of the interview slipping through her fingers. The way that she was starting to sweat was definitely not sexy.

"What do you know?" Morgan asked. The intent focus of her gaze as she stared down Amy made it clear how she'd rose to the top of the wolf-pack. She looked like an apex predator—a sexy, sexy apex predator.

Hold on a minute! Amy was the one who was supposed to be asking the questions here. She straightened her shoulders. Pull it together! You're the one doing the interviewing here, remember? Never show weakness to your subject!

Also, please stop thinking about how hot she is!

"Well, let's start by going through the facts everyone knows," Amy said, tapping her notebook with the end of her pen. "Morgan Rachael Leithe, age 34, born to academic parents in Portland. You rose to the attention of the tech world when you created a revolutionary new sorting algorithm while in the last year of your computer engineering degree, and received millions in venture funding for the app suite that used it. After years of radical growth, you sold it and put that money into green energy tech and investments, starting the Leithe Foundation and soon achieving billionaire status. Not bad progress for the start of your career."

Morgan's face gave nothing away. "Thank you," she said, in the least thankful monotone that Amy had ever heard.

"Then there's many years of new products and philanthropic work, before the big event."

Amy held Morgan's look, her dark brown eyes locked on to that cold blue gaze. "Three years ago, you released a press report to announce your sudden retirement, seemingly unrelated to any occurrence in either the business world or your private life, and sold your stakes in all of your companies. After that, you wrapped up all your affairs and disappeared from the public view altogether. There was speculation about health issues or addiction..."

Amy trailed off, one eyebrow raised expectantly. A silence stretched out. Morgan seemed uninterested in picking up her end of the conversation.

Okay, of course this wasn't going to go easily. Nothing about this assignment had been easy—why would the actual interview be any different?

Amy gave Morgan her best smile. It had been carefully workshopped to say I'm friendly and sympathetic and tooootally not fake, you can definitely trust me. She picked up the conversation starter herself. "But personally, I don't think either of those are the true reason why you left."

That got her attention. Morgan leaned in, her elbows on her knees. "Oh?"

"Yeah." Amy shrugged one shoulder. "There have been way, way worse scandals in the tech world. A secret trip to rehab would be small beans. Secret baby? No problem."

Morgan tapped a finger on the coffee table between them. The dogs followed the gesture like they were watching a tiny tennis match, heads swiveling between Morgan and Amy in rapt attention. "Just because other people have done worse doesn't mean that something wouldn't be embarrassing if it happened to you."

Amy leaned in, mirroring Morgan, narrowing the gap between them. "Embarrassing, sure. Embarrassing enough to ditch an entire empire over? I'm not buying it. You look like you're made of sterner stuff than that."

That seemed to amuse Morgan. "I do, do I?"

"Yep."

"Maybe you're wrong." She placed her hand on her chest, with a smile that had no warmth in it. "Maybe I've got a soft heart."

And maybe pigs will pilot passenger planes. Amy held back a rising sigh of exasperation. She pushed the recorder across the coffee table just a little further in Morgan's direction, and then gave her a smile.

"Then let everyone know about it. Morgan, here's your chance. Why leave? Who betrayed you?"

Morgan opened her mouth, no doubt for more nonsense—but then shut it again. For a moment, she just looked... tired.

For that moment, Amy's hopes rose in her chest like a hot air balloon.

Morgan shrugged nonchalantly. "I got tired of living like that. All the attention, the early starts and long nights... it eventually takes its toll on you. It's a young person's game. I decided to hand over the rat race to the new blood and enjoy my retirement."

The hot air balloon plummeted to Earth and burst into flames.

On paper, what Morgan had said made sense.

Unfortunately, Amy could tell that it was a bunch of crap.

It was all nothing more than rehearsed, boring excuses—and Morgan was holding her gaze, as if daring Amy to call her on it. But if someone was determined to lie to your face like this, what else could you do?

Amy paused, and then decided that the smartest thing to do was to keep playing along. "I see. And what do you spend your time doing, these days?"

Morgan gestured to her surroundings. "I walk my dogs. I paint. I water my plants. It's scenic here. Wouldn't anyone want to throw it all away and live like this?"

"In a town with barely any wifi? No, thank you."

That at least got a snort of laughter from Morgan. The older woman leaned forward, lacing her long fingers together. "Hmm. Tell me about yourself."

"Me?" Amy hesitated. "Well, I work at Zero Nova Media; we're a mixed-medium magazine that mostly covers business and consumer technology news—"

"No, not the company." Morgan looked her in the eyes. "You."

Oookay, this interview was going off of the rails. No, correction: this interview had never been on the rails in the first place, starting from the second Amy got yelled to pieces in the middle of a plate of pancakes. She laughed a little. "Uh, well, there's no big story here. Small town girl wanted to be a journalist, fled to the big city on the ragtag wings of grants and scholarships, and got her big break with Zero Nova. Now..." She spread her hands. "Here I am."

"Sounds like a solid trajectory. You like it there?"

Amy shrugged a shoulder. "No complaints. The boss-lady runs a tight ship, but that just keeps me on my toes."

What was Morgan seeking from all of this? The other woman's expression was unreadable. With a shiver, Amy thought that she definitely never wanted to go up against her in a game of poker.

"When did Zero Nova start up?"

"A few years ago. I was part of the first wave of hires when we were starting up—though I was pretty much just doing page-fillers, puff pieces, and coffee runs back then, hah."

"Ah. The company started after I retired, I see. That explains why I hadn't heard of it until now."

Something jumped out at Amy about that. "Wait... if you've never heard of Zero Nova, why choose us to run your big interview?"

Morgan's pleasant smile was enigmatic. "Shouldn't you already know that?"

Getting a straight answer out of Morgan was about as easy as herding a pack of sugar-hyped toddlers. Amy decided to play simple, and shrugged, offering Morgan a sweet, sheepish smile. "I just do what the boss tells me, Ms. Leithe. She doesn't like it when people ask her too many questions."

"You mustn't be a very good reporter, then," Morgan mused.

A silence fell. The audience of dogs looked from their master to Amy, and then back again, waiting to see who would speak next (and if, perhaps, their words might involve walkies).

Amy was on the opposite side of the planet from her apartment and her job and everything that she held dear. She was tired, and stressed, and dressed in a cheap tourist sweater, and she'd been working herself to death to chase down an interviewee who was clearly delighting in her suffering, and she was on her very last nerve—

And, worse: from the smug little smile on Morgan's face, it looked like the other woman knew it, too.

Maybe this was a test.

Maybe Morgan had never had any intention of giving an interview. It made sense—why break such a long-term seclusion just for a mid-tier magazine?

Or, Amy's mind supplied, maybe Savannah had never actually considered Amy for that promotion. Maybe all of this was just a way to get her out of the way while Georgie got her big break, making her dance for Savannah's amusement to boot.

Either way, it was clear that she was the butt of some joke.

As long as she could keep her life moving forward, her past had no power over her. But as soon as Professional Amy, perfect reporter, stumbled, it was like she was back to being a useless kid all over again.

Yeas had passed since she'd left her past behind. She had a decent collection of small industry awards and nominations for her writing. She had a perfect New York apartment, and a perfect job.

But at that moment, it was like she'd never left home.

Stupid.

Amy shook herself back to reality. Whatever was going on—this interview was clearly going nowhere. Had been going nowhere, in fact, from the moment that their eyes had met across the cafe.

Her watch let her know that she had fifteen minutes before her bus left.

A lot could happen in fifteen minutes.

But here, it clearly wasn't going to.

"Okay, fine," Amy said, her heart pounding. "It's clear that we're done here. I've got all that I need, anyway."

She may have been screaming internally, but Amy hoped that on the outside she looked like a consummate professional as she gathered her equipment and headed back towards the door. Like hell did she want to let Morgan know that she'd won!

Morgan watched her from the other end of the hallway, silent. When Amy got to the door, she turned back to Morgan. "We'll be in touch," she said, with all the haughty professionalism she could muster in her 5'4" frame. "Enjoy your cactus." And I have some ideas on where, exactly, you can put it.

She opened the front door of the cottage... and stared out into nothingness.

She paused, one foot raised.

Um.

Instead of showing Amy a sleepy little New Zealand town, the world outside was one big blank sheet of white. As Amy blinked in shock, tiny pinpricks of cold settled on her face.

A snowstorm?

Morgan made her way over to look outside as well, her extra inches of height letting her look out over the top of Amy like she wasn't even there.

The last thing Amy wanted to do was to let the other woman into her personal space, ruining the excellent drama of the way she'd flounced out, but there wasn't exactly a lot of space in the confines of the hallway.

Huddled together, almost touching, they both stared out into the flurry of snow. With held breaths, they watched fat snowflakes cover the streets outside in a thick white blanket.

"Well, hell," said Morgan, with no small amount of feeling.

"Does this happen a lot?"

"Now and again." Morgan hiked a thumb in the general direction of Mount Doom. "Blizzards come down right off of Ruapehu."

"Shit." Amy caught herself. "I mean, uh—shoot."

Morgan let out a choppy little sound, raspy at the edges, and it took Amy a moment to realize that it was a snort of laughter. She didn't know what she expected Morgan's laugh to sound like, but it wasn't that.

"Listen..." Morgan hesitated. Standing this close to each other, Amy couldn't turn to see her expression, but she could tell from the strain in Morgan's voice that she wasn't exactly happy about what she was about to say next. "Don't go outside right now. It's not safe. Let me make some calls and see when they think it's going to lift."

God, this had ruined such a good dramatic storming off moment! But Morgan was right. Amy stared into the blinding white of the blanket that was settling over Ohakune, and knew that walking out into that was not exactly the smartest idea.

Not that smart ideas were her strength, clearly.

ele

TODAY'S PLANNER:

1pm: You must be tired from all that skiing you did! Take a nap on the bus back to Auckland.

3pm: Grab the airport transfer bus to the airport, check in, and post some airport selfies.

8pm: Catch some Zs on board and wake up when you're back home, secure in a job well done.

TODAY'S PLANNER (AMENDED VERSION)

1pm onwards, sitting in a billionaire's spare bedroom: Um.

Chapter Six

Morgan

"The kitchen's over there, the bathroom's down the hall. The wifi password is borismuffin. Boris, then Muffin. One word, lower case."

"It's... what?"

Morgan pointed at two of her pack. "Boris, and Muffin. I didn't name them, the shelter did. Long passwords are more secure. I rotate through pairs of dog names. Easy to remember, enough characters to be hard to break."

The reporter—Amy—followed her awkwardly down the hallway. "Oh, that's cute."

"Or, at least, I did, anyway. Now that I've told you, I'll have to change that system when you leave."

"Great, thanks for the vote of confidence. Do you get a lot of hackers in a town like this?"

Morgan ignored her. "Don't let the dogs outside even if they bother you; they love playing in the snow, but they need boots to go out in weather like this." Morgan gestured towards a door leading off of the hallway. "This room here is off limits. Don't touch it."

Amy clearly wasn't bothered by such things as tact or manners. "What's in there?"

Morgan rolled her eyes. "It's my art room."

"Painting? Drawing?"

"A bit of everything, whatever catches my interest. I do whatever I want. It's one of the advantages of being retired."

"Are you any good?"

"The dogs haven't criticized me yet."

"Ha."

Morgan led the reporter down the hallway, and then opened the door to the last room. "Here's the guest room. You can set up in here for the time being."

Amy looked through the door at her temporary lodgings... and the pile of boxes and books that were stacked on top of the bed. "Um."

Tendrils of embarrassment began to tease at her, but Morgan refused to be apologetic about the state of her own damn house. "Just move that stuff to the floor."

"You're not worried that I'll rummage through your things?" Amy stepped into the room, then turned and shot her a playful little grin. "What if I uncover all of your dark secrets?"

For a moment back there, Morgan had thought that she'd pushed Amy to her limits. That plastic-perfect smile had faltered, and left something like real emotion in its place. Despite her sweet little face, Amy had looked like she'd wanted to fight.

Then Morgan'd had to make some calls about the snowstorm, and by the time she'd returned, Amy was back to being Savannah's perfect little puppet again.

Morgan was well and truly over perfect people. Whatever small scrap of interest in Amy had popped up inside her was immediately dismissed. All that Morgan needed now was for the snow to lift, so she could send the reporter running off back home.

"If there are any dark secrets that you can winnow out of old coffee-table books," she said, "then you're welcome to them." There. That was Morgan's duties as host fulfilled. "I'll be in the living room if you need me."

"Sure," said Amy. "If you need me, I'll be here trying to coordinate calls across time zones that don't want to play nice together." She lifted one of the books from the pile and used it to give Morgan a little salute. "And, if that doesn't work out, I'll apparently be learning about the ins and outs of Peruvian llama raising."

ele

Morgan sat on the armchair, her book in her hand. Detective Reuben Reid, hard-bitten sleuth and part-time vampire hunter, was closing in on the villain of the novel. The heiress to the coal-mine fortune had disappeared, but he'd been able to find a vital clue—

From the other side of the house, someone coughed.

Morgan jumped, and then ground her teeth. She went back to her book.

Reid threw the door of the abandoned lumber mill open, knowing that the clue that he'd uncovered at the scene would lead him straight to the culprit, but was he in the nick of time? He rounded the corner—

There was the sound of someone starting a phone conversation, their words muffled but the cadence of their speech loud enough to hear through the walls.

—he rounded the corner, and as the scent of blood pricked at his vampire-hunting senses, Reid pulled out his pistol and kicked a door down—

There was the creak of floorboards. As Morgan stared into space, they started squeaking in a repeating pattern as someone began to walk around the guest room. Left, to where Morgan knew the window was. Right, back to the door. Left. Right.

Morgan slammed her book shut.

Morgan had had a roommate in college, back in the day. It had been an adventure of noise-cancelling headphones and spaces clearly demarcated —my stuff on this side, yours on that side—and then intensely cold silences when things began to creep over the lines. After that point, she'd pointedly lived alone. No housemates. No partners. Just her, and a series of fully-serviced luxury apartments, with everything exactly the way that she liked it.

As she'd grown a little older and become less interested in having the newest toys and the shiniest things, she'd learned that she didn't need the luxury apartment side of the deal—but she still needed to live alone.

What kind of sociopath would actually enjoy having someone else around all the time? That was completely beyond her.

The dogs, flopped out over their couches and beds as per usual, looked up at her, uncertainty visible in the tilts of their heads and the pricks of their ears. Another person? In the house? Boris picked up a rope tug-toy, looking towards the hallway and the guest bedroom beyond. Do they want to play?

No, Morgan thought, bitterly, they don't want to play. They want to make an inordinate amount of noise, and then pick through my personal life like a hyena with a carcass.

The phone conversations were muffled by the thick walls between the two of them, but they seemed like they were going to go on for a long time. After it became clear that the small cottage's peace and quiet was going to be thoroughly ruined for the near future, Morgan gave up on her book.

She looked out the window, judging the snowfall. The Antarctic blast of the afternoon had been blowing for hours, but at the moment, it had dwindled to a persistent but light snowfall.

It was only a small lull, and Morgan knew from experience that it was bound to pick up sooner or later—but even a small lull was enough. Morgan got to her feet, the newest Detective Reid novel reluctantly set to the side for the moment, and made her way down the hallway.

The door to the guest room was open. Inside, the reporter was sitting cross-legged on the bed, in the middle of some sort of impromptu command center—phone pressed to her ear, laptop in front of her, tablet and paper notes spread out around her like a spread of tarot cards. For a moment, she looked less like a weapon of destruction sent to hurt Morgan, and more like an ordinary woman, stressed out by work. Frowning at something on the phone, Amy chewed idly on the edge of her thumbnail.

Morgan rapped her knuckles on the doorframe, and then when Amy looked up, hitched a thumb over her shoulder. I'm going out, she mouthed.

The kid looked at her in visible confusion and mouthed back In the snow?, but then the muffled sound of someone lecturing Amy began to kick up over the phone. Amy shot Morgan a wry, apologetic look, and then went back to her work. She plastered on the slightly manic smile of someone who's been neck-deep in unpleasant phone calls for far too long, and can't yet see the end of them in sight. "Yes, hi, I'm still here, yes..."

Morgan left her to it.

eee

New Zealand was sometimes called Australia's Canada, and there were some apt parallels. Politics that leaned more toward the left, colder weather, and picturesque alpine scenery: it wasn't a bad comparison.

Thankfully, that comparison didn't extend to the amount of snow that the country got. Instead of the multiple-foot-deep drifts of snow that a Canadian snowstorm would have dropped, the blizzard had so far left a foot or two covering the town.

Despite not being all that much, that was still deep enough to close out the single road that led out of town, with no snow-plow desperate enough to try to clear the long winding drive from Ohakune to the nearest big town while it was still falling. The plan, as it always was with this sort of thing, was to wait things out.

On foot, it was still shallow enough for someone to wade through, if they were patient enough to go slow and determined enough to get somewhere. Morgan, spurred on by the deep discomfort of having someone in her house, was both.

Ohakune was small, and Morgan had lived in it long enough to be able to navigate her way through the streets in a snowfall. Rugged up in her snow gear, she waded her way across the streets towards the town's emergency gathering point: the visitor's center.

A few dozen people were mulling around inside the center. The room was full of the low rumble of conversation, interrupted by the occasional laugh.

When Morgan stepped inside, the conversations stuttered to a halt.

No-one was rude enough to outright stare at her—at least, not these days. That didn't actually make the awkward silence that surrounded her wherever she went in this small town feel any better. Keeping her expression neutral, Morgan stepped inside, joining the small gathering.

And immediately regretted doing so.

"I thought this was a meeting for locals."

"Shoosh, mum!"

Marie, certified Cranky Old Witch, did not shoosh, no matter the pleading looks that Kaia, her daughter, was giving her. She gave Morgan a critical look. "Isn't that what community means? And this is a community meeting, isn't it?"

This was something that Morgan was used to. It was true that she had never exactly managed to fit into the small town community—but if people wanted to make a fuss about it, then that was their problem, not hers. She ignored the other woman, and kept her attention on the front of the room. Marie let out a little snort of laughter, and Morgan knew that it meant I knew it.

Morgan stared ahead at the front of the room, at a woman who was currently climbing up on to a chair, and ignored the way that she could hear Marie and Kaia whispering about her to her side.

"All right, listen up," said the deputy mayor, once she'd managed to clamber on top of the chair. She clapped her hands for the small audience to pay attention. "Here's the deal. This blizzard was supposed to miss us, but shit happens, hey? According to the weather report, it looks like it'll be in town for a few days."

There were a few groans from the audience, but for the most part, the town's unexpected guest was accepted with a certain level of begrudging practicality. This was not anyone's first snowy rodeo. When a surprise snowstorm turned up every few years, everyone was fairly used to hunkering down and riding it out. There were plenty of upsides about living so close to such a beautiful mountain range, and so the downsides that came with that were usually worth it.

"D'you think the roads'll be open by tomorrow?" Kaia asked. "I have a booth at a farmers' market lined up."

"Nope. Don't even think about it. Stay home, stay warm, stay safe. If I catch anyone trying to drive in this, I'll go straight to the highest authority: I'll tell your mums."

That got a round of chuckles from the crowd.

"Does everyone have enough food and firewood for the next few days? Gas, medications, water? Will everyone check on their neighbors when they can? Okay, great. If something comes up, we can talk over Facebook. I'll start a group."

Everyone murmured in vague agreement. Morgan hesitated, about to ask about what to do if you didn't have a Facebook—and then gave up.

No-one who had seen the backend of Facebook's data-gathering operations had a Facebook themselves. In Silicon Valley, it was a common enough thing: people would happily promote their businesses on Facebook, but they wouldn't have one themselves. Morgan was no exception. What did she want with social media, anyway? She'd gone to a lot of effort to make herself disappear, after all. She wasn't about to undo all of that hard work just to play Farmville.

Still, though, she wasn't in Silicon Valley any more. Outside of that little bubble, not having social media cut you off from the people around you.

"Okay, people! Does anyone have anything else to bring up? Any questions, problems?"

The blizzard was going to take days to clear. That meant days of someone else being inside Morgan's little house—and not just anyone: a reporter specifically sent to pick through Morgan's new life.

The idea of it was unfathomable. Utterly terrible. Morgan needed to do something.

All she needed to say was Can anyone take in the American reporter?

One sentence. The town was full of generous people with spare rooms. All she had to do was to speak up now, and in a matter of seconds, the reporter would be out of her hair for good. Everyone would be polite to her to her face about it, and then they'd get back to talking to their friends.

They'd probably love to take her in. Amy was a source of new, exciting gossip. They could pump her for information: who is this Leithe, anyway? Why is she so stuck-up? Any juicy gossip you can share?

Morgan's chest felt heavy.

The seconds ticked on.

"That's that, then." The deputy mayor climbed down off of her chair. "Enjoy the next few days, folks. They're going to be cozy ones."

Chapter Seven

Amy

"What do you mean you don't know?"

The woman on the other end of the phone sounded bored. "You're going to have to take it up with the sky, ma'am. We can't know for sure when the snow will stop. Until we get the all-clear, all roads are closed, and all buses are cancelled."

Amy chewed her thumbnail—and then caught herself, frowning. She'd thought she'd left that particular bad habit behind years ago. Old Amy had been a nailbiter; professional new Amy was too cool under pressure to do something so childish.

"There's not a single road out of here?"

"None that you'd want to risk a landslide on. Sorry, ma'am."

She thought about all those lush green hills that the bus had passed through on the way into Ohakune, winding between them on narrow little roads. At the time, they'd looked gorgeous. Scenic! Now, though, Amy shuddered to think about those rolling hills closing in over the roads, like an open book shutting with a snap.

"Okay, okay, I get the picture."

The woman on the line made a vague and entirely insincere noise of customer-service sympathy. "We'll let you know when we get the all-clear to restart our services. What's the best number to reach you on?"

After a few minutes of administrative details and platitudes, Amy hung up.

On the upside, the snowstorm was probably only going to keep her delayed for a few days—a week, tops. Right? Amy wasn't an expert on New Zealand, but she was fairly sure that its inhabitants didn't disappear underneath blizzards for months at a time.

All of her missed flights were on the company dime, and the company would be the one dealing with travel insurance, not her. So, when you think about it... it was kind of like a free ski vacation, just without the skiing, right?

On the downside, she was going to be stuck with Morgan for the near future. All the accommodation in town was booked out. Amy had checked out of her room in the morning, and other tourists had come in in the afternoon, before the storm had hit.

On the upside, that gave her plenty of time to pump Morgan for more interview facts! Also: sleeping in a billionaire's guest bedroom? Not too shabby. As someone who'd done their share of couch-crashing and sleeping on cheap air mattresses in her college days, it was definitely not the worst bed to have to sleep on in a pinch—though it was clearly one that didn't get much use. Amy had had to move a haphazard collection of books and boxes off of the bed to make room for herself, and thought it was as clean and dusted as the rest of the house, it still had the aura of a space that didn't get a lot of use. Not a lot of sleepovers were happening in chez Leithe, Amy guessed.

On the downside of being snowed in... she was going to be stuck with Morgan for the near future. Awkwaaard.

Amy threw her head back and sighed, slithering bonelessly down against the headboard.

After that failure of an interview, she'd spent the rest of the day on her phone and in her inbox, to very little result. She couldn't do much on her end, and HR and Zero Nova's admin team couldn't do much from their end, so everyone was currently just chasing their tails trying to find a way to get Amy out of there. As far as Amy could tell, there wasn't one. She was just going to have to sit there and wait.

Waiting wasn't exactly her strong suit.

Uncaring of how she'd wasted the hours, the ever-present swarm of dogs nuzzled at her hands. After Morgan had left, they'd appeared around the edge of the open door, noses poking in until Amy had called them over. She resigned herself to booping their damp little snoots.

"Are you Boris?" she asked one of the bigger dogs, and then looked down towards the broad little pitbull. "Or is that you, buddy? You look like you could be a Boris."

She flipped the name tag that was on its collar. It said, in careful and precise engraving, Orange Juice.

She snorted. Okay, despite the icy, haughty impression that she seemed to like to give, apparently Morgan wasn't all business.

Amy ruffled an assortment of furry ears. When she'd first arrived, the constantly-shifting mass of dogs had been too much for her to keep track of—even if she hadn't been distracted by meeting Morgan for the first time.

Now, though, she was starting to get used to them. There were the two big ones, and then the two smaller ones, and then, to her surprise, there was...

Outside the open door, the fifth dog, a little white mop on legs, wandered past down the cottage's hallway, doing its own thing.

"Hi, girl!" Amy stretched out a hand. "C'mere, let me meet you."

The dog gave her a withering look, and then turned and continued on its way.

Ouch. Blanked by a dog.

Still, the fifth dog was clearly an outlier. The rest of the pack made up a happy, friendly little tornado of wagging tails and perky ears, eager to spend time with her.

Or, at least, eager for any treats that they could shake out of her. The terrier took that opportunity to stick its nose in her pocket, wuffling happily.

"Hey! I still don't have any treats, guys," Amy groaned, and shooed them away. Apparently disgusted with the lack of manners of this new houseguest, the dogs began to mosey off, leaving her alone.

Alone in the house of someone who wanted her gone, with a job that she couldn't do.

Amy put her face in her hands, and groaned. She took a deep breath, and then ran her hands from her face over her hair, shaking herself.

I was betrayed.

Morgan's words kept running through her mind. Had it been a business deal gone wrong? Many people had benefited from Morgan stepping down, but no one person seemed to stand out. Had it been a team effort, secret handshakes behind the scenes coming together to force her out? It wouldn't have been the first time in history, and it sure wouldn't be the last. But, still: why leave absolutely everything behind, then?

Or had it been something else? Something more personal?

As far as Amy had been able to tell—and she'd done as much digging as she could—Morgan had never been romantically involved with anyone. Oh, there had been a few rumors, now and again, but those sorts of things just seemed to spontaneously pop up around famous people, like mushrooms after rain. Especially if those famous people happened to be women. Secret toyboys, secret weddings, secret babies—Amy wasn't sure how the average celebrity was supposed to make time for all these secret lives. She barely had time for her own life!

Amy had rifled through those articles and blind items, but at the end, she hadn't put much faith in them. Morgan happening to be in the same photo as another tech celeb, Morgan standing close to someone at a gala... Amy had recognized the attempts of someone trying to spin a story out of nothing when she saw it, and she had dismissed them all.

Whatever had gone on behind Morgan's decision to step down, it was something deeper.

And she was going to find out what that was.

...As soon as Morgan came back, that was.

Idly, Amy got out her planner, and flipped it to the current week. Every single day had been covered in prospective plans, and every single one of those plans had promptly been scratched out and replaced. Instead of looking like a sensible professional's schedule, her planner looked like something that the main character in a thriller might find in a madman serial killer's apartment.

She had crossed out "make action plan with work" "make escape plan" "drill Morgan for details". Instead, at a loss for anything else to do, in their place she had simply written "wait".

So, taking a breath, she picked up the nearest book, and she waited.

And waited.

And waited.

Just as she was starting to plot her next Facebook post (poor me! all alone with nothing but llama facts to keep me company!), there was a noise from the other end of the house. From the guest room, Amy heard the sounds of Morgan coming back inside.

There were the scrabbling of little paws as the horde of dogs hurried over to their mom, tails smacking against the walls and furniture now and again. There was a little sound of greeting as Morgan said her hellos to them, and thumps as she kicked the snow off of her boots. The door latched, then had to be latched again—Morgan swore at the door frame, the old bones of the cottage having warped in the cold weather. There was the sound of Morgan leaning against the door, and then sighing deeply.

Then, unexpectedly, came the sound of humming.

Amy held her breath as she heard Morgan begin to potter around her own home, humming to herself. It was the sort of vague little singsong tune that people made to themselves when they were alone, never intended to be overheard by anyone except for the dogs and the houseplants.

Amy hadn't lived with anyone else in a long time. It was strange to hear someone else inside the house with you, going about their own personal business.

It was cozy, in a way. It felt... nice.

She curled up on the bed, tucking her besocked feet underneath her, and listened to Morgan make her way through the cottage.

The polite thing to do, she knew would be to announce her presence. Hey, Earth to Morgan, there's still a reporter stashed in your spare room, remember?

But this... this was too cute to ruin.

After a moment, though, Morgan rounded the corner. When she clapped eyes on Amy through the opened guest room door, she jumped a little in alarm, the song dying instantly.

"Not used to having guests?"

Morgan seemingly recovered with grace, but there was the tiniest hint of color in her cheeks. "You could say that." She looked over at Amy, sitting on the bed, and then at the empty bedside table that was next to her. "You haven't been making yourself hot drinks? It's freezing."

"Oh, uh..." Amy laughed a little at herself, embarrassed at being caught out. "I didn't want to intrude," she confessed.

There was just something so intimate at poking through someone's house, even their kitchen. After Morgan had left that morning, going to talk to the other townspeople, Amy had spent a few minutes in the kitchen, feeling awkward as she'd peeked into the pantry. The sight of a hand-made mug, with a messy thumbprint in the ceramic where Morgan had clearly struggled to attach the handle, had filled Amy with a sense somewhere between second-hand embarrassment and unbearable fondness, and made her decide that she didn't need a coffee that badly, after all; she'd grabbed some muesli bars and fled.

Not that she was stupid enough to open her mouth and say any of that.

Morgan quirked an eyebrow at her anyway. "I thought reporters liked rummaging around in peoples' business."

"The details of their personal lives? Sure. The contents of their mug cupboard? Nope. That's a pass from me."

Morgan rolled her eyes and jerked her chin toward the rest of the house, in what was unmistakably a command. She left the room without bothering to see if Amy would obey her.

God, what an ego. Still... why not follow her? It wasn't like refreshing her inbox yet again was going to make anything helpful appear.

Amy pocketed her phone and followed Morgan's command, for the moment as obedient as one of the dogs. When Morgan pointed at an armchair in the living room, she slithered into it. A few minutes of clattering and kettle-whistling later, Morgan reappeared from the kitchen with two cups of hot chocolate, and slid one Amy's way across the coffee table with an expression that said don't even try to turn this down, kid. Amy obliged.

"This all must be terribly dull for you." Morgan took a sip of her drink, and then gestured around the room. "What do you do for fun back home?"

"Netflix, drink, and sleep."

Morgan paused. "No, I meant... hobbies? Pastimes?"

"What? I'm in journalism, I don't have time for hobbies." Amy laughed. "I have my career to focus on."

That seemed to disturb Morgan. She cocked her head to the side, one eyebrow raised archly. Amy was getting to hate that look, like Amy was a creature in a petri dish being studied.

"Even busy people need hobbies," Morgan said. "I'm no stranger to journalists, and all the ones that I know had plenty of personal interests."

"Maybe that was true back in the old days, but not now."

"The old—the old days?" Morgan scowled. "I haven't been out of the game that long."

"Hey, things change fast. And I'm not risking getting my work outsourced to overseas content farms just so I can take time to..." Amy shrugged. "Play basketball? Sing? Play the tuba? Whatever it is that people with free time do."

There was a moment of silence. "Well," Morgan said, her expression hard to read. "That sounds depressing." Then, like she'd ruled the conversation to be over, she picked a well-thumbed paperback up off of a nearby bookshelf, and opened it back up to her bookmark.

Clearly, that was the extent of her interest in Amy.

Amy opened her mouth to keep the conversation going, ready to innocently dig for information, but Morgan turned a page and took a sip.

Okay. Okay. Amy knew a dismissal when she saw one.

Amy had been sent half-way around the world to find Morgan; it would have been rude to tell her to get bent. Instead, her cheeks heating with something that was half made of irritation and half made of shame, Amy stood up from her chair. "Thanks for the drink," she said, and headed back to the guest room.

Morgan waved one hand silently, not bothering to look up.

Amy did not storm back to her room. It would have been childish and beneath her. Instead, she walked very professionally back to her room, where she very professionally picked up a pillow, and then very professionally swore a blue streak into it.

That done, and feeling at least a little bit better, Amy turned her attention back down to her laptop, and got back to the file that contained her article.

Well, the little of it that she'd managed to put together, anyway. A description of Morgan's new life was only going to fill so many paragraphs.

The readers were going to want juicy details. So far, all the material that Amy had to fill the pages with was that Morgan was an asshole with too many dogs, and some thrilling facts about cacti.

She took a sip of her drink. She also makes a nice hot chocolate.

Unless she could figure out how to get Morgan to crack and actually talk to her before the snowstorm settled, that was all that she'd have for Savannah.

Somehow, she needed to bust this whole story wide open.

ele

The next few hours were spent in a mix of boring emergency paperwork and working on the world's roughest rough draft. Outside, feathery snow piled on the windowsill, forming round little miniature drifts. Slowly, the world outside the cottage began to dim, the sun dipping behind the pine trees.

Just as Amy was busy trying to figure out if Morgan had any weak points (signs were not looking promising), yet another email notification finally popped up. It was Savannah, continuing that day's back-and-forth over Amy's travel details.

Use the company card as much as you need, but keep receipts (and no, like I reminded you last time, cocktails aren't work expenses). HR will hook you up with whatever you need, so keep them apprised of any changes and let them know when the roads open. Your accommodation is able to extend your stay, I assume. Don't slack off.

Amy bought her hands up to type her response—but then paused.

In the messy scramble to sort everything out, certain facts had been left out. As far as Savannah knew, Amy was still in the bed and breakfast she'd initially been staying in.

Did she really want to tell her boss that she was staying with her source? Sleeping in a billionaire's guest bedroom, and playing with her dogs? She chewed her lip. There was nothing wrong with it, really. It was strange, sure, but there was no reason to lie.

Still, something about it made her uneasy. She didn't want anyone to know about this.

Cocktails can be an important workplace expense under the right circumstances, she typed back. Will do. Yes, boss. Yes, boss. No, boss.

Amy stared at her technically-not-a-lie on the screen, and then pressed send.

Someone cleared their throat.

Amy jumped. Morgan stood behind the open door, staring down at Amy with boardroom boss bitch vibes. Normally Amy would have appreciated being on the receiving end of a look like that in the bedroom, but not at that precise moment. Amy swallowed, like she was a student who'd got caught playing truant.

"Well, I'm not cooking for you," Morgan announced, like that made any sense.

"Ye-es?" Amy managed.

"And I don't want you ruining my cast iron pans," Morgan continued, "and no-one's going to be delivering food out in this weather." She looked down at Amy, and then, in her flat monotone, gave the least romantic delivery of a romantic line that Amy had ever heard. "Would you like to have dinner with me?"

Belatedly, Amy realized exactly how late it was getting. Her stomach, which had been powered down under the stress of dealing with landslides and workplace emails, powered back up with a wobbly little growl. Amy pressed a hand to it, embarrassed. "Uh, sure. But... out there? It's still snowing, right?"

"It isn't far," Morgan said. "We won't get lost."

If that was coming from anyone else, Amy would have guaranteed that they were headed for doomed headlines like Hot Billionaire And Plucky Reporter Freeze To Death Trying To Find Nearest Micky Ds. Morgan looked like she had better things to do than freeze, though—and probably better taste than to spring for McDonalds, to boot. Amy got to her feet. "Sure, okay. Where are we headed?"

"Nowhere, dressed like that." Morgan hitched a thumb over her shoulder. "Follow me."

Without any grounds for an objection, Amy let herself be led to the mudroom, where Morgan proceeded to rifle through a collection of jackets piled on a hat stand. "You'll need some cold-weather clothes," she explained, then held one up to Amy, squinting. "Do you think you'll fit in my gear?"

"Wow, asking a girl out to dinner and then calling her fat? Way harsh, Morgan."

Amy had just been joking, the sort of reflexive back-and-forth she was used to with Georgie, but Morgan didn't seem to realize. Her eyes widened in alarm—the first ungraceful move that Amy had seen her make—and she froze in place. "I didn't—I mean, I was just..."

Oh my god, Morgan could be cute. What? Amy half wanted to keep the moment going, seeing how far she could push the other woman, but her sense of mercy eventually won out. "It's fine," she laughed. "I was just playing around! It'll fit."

She slid her arms into the jacket that Morgan, frozen by awkwardness, was still holding up to her. It was long on her—Morgan was a good five inches taller, and though snow gear was naturally bulky, Amy still felt a little like she was wearing an oversized boyfriend hoodie. "See?"

Morgan cleared her throat, and then looked away. "Don't waste time," she groused, "it's only going to get colder out there." Without ceremony, she pulled a pair of gloves and a hat from a box, and nearly threw them at Amy.

It took all of Amy's people-skills training to not laugh at the look on Morgan's face. Solemnly, she slid the snow gloves on, and pulled on the hat. It had a little rainbow pom-pom on top. Amy could not imagine Morgan wearing a specific piece of clothing less than this one, but here it was.

She was learning a lot about Morgan, she discovered.

Was any of it helpful for her article? Nope.

Was it intriguing anyway? Definitely.

ele

Following Morgan, Amy let herself be led out into the cold of the night.

Snow was still falling, but at least it was now falling vertically, like snow should, rather than the harsh horizontal blizzard snow that had first blanketed the town.

The yellow of the streetlamps didn't do much but divide the world into light and dark halves: the light, showing everything covered in a thick layer of snow; the dark: hiding everything else, swallowed up by the winter night.

With only the two of them in sight, it felt as if they were the only people left in the world. The snow muffled every sound except the groaning creaks of the pine boughs as they bent under their winter weights, and the crunch beneath their boots as the two of them penguin-marched across the street.

"It's so quiet," Amy marveled.

Morgan looked over at her. "You haven't spent time in snow before?"

"Not really." Amy shook her head, and then laughed a little at the sight of the flakes showering off of her hat. "I grew up in the backwaters of Arizona, not a lot of snow there. Then I moved to New York, and yeah, it snows there, but not, like..." She gestured to the pristine white that covered the ground and draped over the pine trees that lined the streets and trailed up into the mountain. "Not like this. It's like something out of a fairy-tale."

In the quiet of the night, it was easy to hear the soft raspy sound of Morgan's laughter. "This is a magical part of the world," she said, with fondness in her voice. Then, rather less romantically, she said, "Watch out for the curb," and gestured at a point on the ground that, to Amy's untrained eyes, seemed the same as any other point of snow. Morgan offered her hand, and Amy automatically reached out to accept it, letting Morgan guide her to step upwards and carefully find the curb that was hidden underneath the snow.

"Thanks."

"Don't mention it." Morgan jerked her chin forward. "It's just around the trees here. Just step where I do."

Through the thick padding of the snow gloves, it was impossible to feel someone else's body heat. Still, Amy could almost swear that she could feel a touch of warmth on her fingertips where Morgan had taken her hand.

— ℓℓℓ —

Morgan's goal really did turn out to be close. A few minutes later, Amy was standing in the doorway to the Red Deer Lodge.

It turned out to be a warm, noisy restaurant, modeled in sturdy wood and deer antlers, with a hearty hearth fire roaring away on the far wall. As soon as Amy had pried herself out of Morgan's borrowed clothes and hung them on a hook in the entranceway, she hustled over to its side. The heat soothed the chill from her nose and ears, and she let out a near-orgasmic sigh as she bathed in its glow.

"God, I needed that."

"Any closer to the fire and you'll be in it," Morgan chuckled. She tilted her chin towards the tables. "Let's sit. They do a good spiced mead when it gets cold. That'll warm you up."

"I have never wanted anything more," Amy said with feeling, and let herself be led over to a table. She thought about the minor panic that she'd sent Morgan into over the jacket, and grinned as Morgan sat down.

"What, you're not going to pull my seat out for me? What kind of date is this?"

Morgan stared at her again, that unexpected tinge of panic in her expression again. How fun! This time, though, she seemed to have calibrated somewhat to Amy's teasing, and recovered in a moment. "One that ends with you being tossed out into the snow, if you're not careful," she warned.

"Ouch. Duly noted."

Despite the snow, the restaurant was quite busy. Amy looked over the crowd, and noticed some familiar faces. "Oh, hey, it's Marie and Kaia."

She waved to them, getting a smile and nod in return—then noticed that Morgan didn't do the same. "Bad blood?" she ventured.

Morgan blinked at her. "What?"

"The locals." Amy gave Morgan's elbow a careful nudge: just enough to be friendly, but not so friendly to wind up with her being thrown out into a snowdrift. "Is there some small-town drama going on? You can tell me. Not even in an interviewer way—just a small-town girl way."

"Is that so?"

Amy's eyes sparkled with amusement. "Yeah. You should have seen some of the feuds back home, they could have put Game of Thrones to shame. Someone's great-grandma once stole someone else's great-grand-aunt's man, and eighty years later people are cussing each other out in a Walmart parking lot."

"Ha." Morgan shook her head. "No, no real feuds, no blood, bad or good." She looked into her mead for a moment, and then shrugged. "I just don't know them very well."

Oh? That seemed strange. Amy thought back over what she'd learned about Morgan so far. "Did you settle down in Ohakune straight away, or are you a newbie here?"

"Straight away, more or less." Morgan took a sip. "I knew what I was looking for: privacy, nature, clean air. Somewhere with a good quality of life." She wrinkled her nose. "No spiders, too. That's a bonus. Australia got ruled out right at the start. No amount of sun is worth dealing with that."

Okay, Amy was firmly with Morgan on that count. But one thing was strange about what she'd just heard.

Morgan had been in town for years, and still didn't know anyone?

Amy knew from her research that Morgan Leithe could walk into a boardroom of a hostile company and walk out with their CEOs seamlessly merged into her flock, without bruised egos getting in the way. She could give inspirational talks all day without missing a beat. She was a consummate professional, never ruffled, always able to get what she wanted.

But she couldn't talk to her neighbors? Amy had already received Facebook requests from most of the people she'd talked to in town—though to be fair, a good percentage of those were from the many different accounts of the backpacker trio, and their metal band, and their page for their yoga class side-hustle, and their discussion group that was campaigning for the legality of certain kinds of plants.

Something was clearly up, and Amy was going to get to the bottom of it.

She sipped her mead with a smile. She'd always wanted to say that.

What followed over dinner wasn't quite easy conversation, but at least it was better than the stop-start tempo of their previous attempts at talking. Sometime between Amy's enquiries of if Morgan had seen any good movies lately (no) or followed a sports team (no) or been anywhere interesting recently (three guesses, and the first two didn't count), the food thankfully arrived: a steaming hot plate of venison stew for Morgan, and a hearty lasagna for Amy.

Amy eyed the plate of bambi on Morgan's side of the table. "You know, for some reason, I just assumed you'd be a vegetarian."

Morgan raised an eyebrow, her fork raised. "Why?"

Amy shrugged. "I don't know. You just kind of have that vibe. Maybe it's all the arts and crafts."

That earned her one of Morgan's low chuckles. "I don't think you know as much about me as you think you do. No," she continued, "I'm not a vegetarian. Besides, deer are pests here. I'd rather this country was less full of them, and more full of kakapo."

"Sorry, what?"

"Kakapo?" Morgan looked a little surprised. "A type of bird here."

Amy squinted. "I thought that was a kiwi. You know, like the fruit."

Distracted by Amy's silliness, Morgan let a small smile slip through her ice queen artifice. It looked good on her. "No—well, yes, that's another one. It's a different bird." She held her hands out, about the size of a football. "Endangered. They're in all the tourism materials these days, I'm surprised you didn't see anything about them on the way over."

"Uh, I can just about tell a seagull from a sparrow, if I'm lucky. David Attenborough, I'm not." Amy laughed. "Besides, I didn't come here for a vacation. Someone else booked my tickets and all. No bird-watching adventures for Amy."

"Oh, that's a shame. You should definitely go and see them, when you get the chance."

"Have you seen them?"

Morgan paused. "Well, not yet, but one day—"

"Oh? Do as I say, not as I do?" Amy teased. "Well, maybe we should go together, then," she said. "You show me this rare endangered football bird, and I'll make appropriate ooh and ahh noises."

Morgan scoffed at her, but she looked like she was trying not to smile.

The conversation continued until Amy was stuffed, her plate thoroughly cleaned. A roaring hot fire, a belly full of good food, and a glass full of mead. Snow falling outside, like a fairy-tale. Amy's eyes fell half-lidded with satisfaction, and she sighed in contentment.

"So this is what you gave up everything for, huh?" she said without thinking.

Morgan's expression closed up like a bear trap. "What do you mean by that?"

"Nothing?" Amy frowned. "I'm just... making conversation."

"Sure you are." Morgan's glare could have cut glass.

Belatedly, Amy realized what was happening. Morgan thought this had all been an act to get her to open up?

Amy had accidentally stepped on a landmine. She tried to walk it back. "Not everything is about the interview—"

"If that's what you think, then you're not a particularly good reporter."

"Oh my god." Amy ground her teeth. "Fine then, so what? That's what I'm here for, anyway. That's what you wanted me here for. I didn't have to come half-way around the world to be insulted."

God! Amy had had it with this nightmare of a woman and her bizarre hot-and-cold temper. "I'll head back and leave you to it," she said peevishly, and reached to dig her wallet out of her purse. "I'll put this on the company card."

It was a snide little gesture, sure, but for some reason Morgan reacted like Amy had reached over the table and slapped her. "I'll pay for myself, thank you very much," she snapped, her voice dripping ice. She shoved her chair back, getting to her feet with military crispness.

In a moment, Amy was left behind at the table, Morgan's figure retreating out the door and into the snow, a repeat of the scene at the cafe.

She stared down at their half-empty mead glasses, frowning.

What the hell had just happened?

ele

When Amy made her way back to Morgan's house, following her footprints in the snow, the porch light was on, but the rest of the lights in the house were off. She opened the door with a strange, claustrophobic feeling—it was like she was sneaking in guiltily, giving her flashbacks to coming home after a night spent out past curfew.

Still, there was no sound, even when she had to jam the ill-fitting front door shut with a thump to get it to stay closed. The door to Morgan's room was shut, and the light inside seemed to be off.

She trailed her fingers against the walls of the hallways until she found the guest room, then turned on the light, stepped inside, and shut the door behind her. Once she was back in her room, she slumped back against the door, letting out a sigh.

Alone in her empty room, Amy wished that she could have stayed talking about frivolous things.

Chapter Eight

Morgan

As a life rule, Morgan had avoided awkward morning-afters. She'd never woken up next to someone unfortunate, and she'd never had to try to feign politeness as she palmed them off.

So to find herself having to go through a similar rigmarole at the age of 34, and without even the benefit of having slept with them first—it galled.

"I have this," Morgan said, flipping her omelet.

"Sure," Amy replied, her voice breezy. The reporter had appeared that morning half-way into Morgan's morning routine, throwing her off. Despite the early hour, she had her regular professional face of makeup on, seeming more like she was about to head in front of news cameras than bumble around in a cozy little cottage kitchen.

Amy hadn't said anything about the spat in the Lodge. Morgan was wary, but she wasn't going to bring it up if the other woman wasn't. What was there to say, anyway—sorry for the lapse, I temporarily forgot that you're the enemy? Instead, they'd both moved on as if it had never happened.

The pressure of presumed politeness had made Morgan, caught out in the middle of already making breakfast for herself, unwillingly volunteer to make an omelet for Amy, too. Instead of that making her go away, though, Amy now roamed back and forth through the kitchen, opening cupboards and drawers.

Morgan had to lean out of the way as she went, dodging elbows and trying not to bump her. She had never thought of her kitchen as small before, but now she felt unexpectedly constrained by the presence of another person.

"What plates is your favorite? Green, cream, the ones with the little kiwi birds painted on—"

"Any."

"You want juice or coffee?"

"Don't touch my coffee machine."

"So—juice then?"

Morgan turned to glare at her. "What are you doing?"

"Uh, getting out the crockery?" Amy looked up in honest confusion. "You know, helping?"

"I don't need help in my own kitchen." Morgan winced internally at how defensive she sounded. "Go sit in the living room."

For once, Amy didn't say anything, which Morgan appreciated. She did, however, raise her eyebrows in a certain way, which Morgan very much did not.

Morgan grit her teeth. "What?"

"Nothing." But Amy's expression said that there was something rattling around in that unhappily sharp mind of hers, and a moment later she opened her mouth again with a wry little smile. "I just wondered how you managed to take over mergers with manners like this."

Morgan viciously stabbed her spatula into the omelet. "People change."

"Yes, but the question is why. Let me guess... you joined a cult? No, then you'd be spreading the gospel of your new pyramid scheme savior. Hmm. Terrible cocaine habit? No, that usually makes people talk more, not less."

"Knock it off."

"I have to come up with something." Amy leant one hip against the cupboard. "People have questions. I'm here to answer them, after all." She twirled a tea-towel. "And if I don't get actual answers, I'll have to supply speculation instead..."

Without missing a beat, Morgan slid the entire omelet that she was making for Amy on top of her own plate, double-stacking it on top of her own breakfast, and then began to carry it away.

Amy let out a squeak of distress. "Hey! You can't leave me to starve!"

"You won't. There's muesli bars in the cupboard."

"Some host."

"Some reporter," Morgan shot back. "I thought interviewers were supposed to develop rapport with their subjects instead of antagonizing them."

"Well, some subjects are more open to that kind of thing than others." Amy gave Morgan a foxy smile, charmingly crooked. "If you want to be friends, let's break out a board game. I'm a shark at Scrabble."

The expression was so familiar. The sight of it made something in Morgan's chest hurt. Grinding her teeth, Morgan made her way to the living room. Ignoring Amy, she sat in her favorite chair, and put the regretfully tall plate of omelets down on the coffee table.

Amy dropped into the armchair opposite Morgan.

Morgan glared. "What are you doing?"

"Working on the interview, as you so kindly suggested that I do."

"Uh-huh. Do you have much for it so far?"

"Well, let me check my notes: you disappeared, and now you're here, in the most boring town on the planet, doing nothing. Eating my breakfast to punish me. That's it, that's the entirety of my notes."

"I'm doing a lot of different things."

"Nothing that anyone will want to buy a magazine to find out about." Amy cocked her head. "Unless I ditch my current gig and shop this article to an arts and crafts mag instead. Spill the beans on your secret life as an amateur potter."

"I don't think your boss would approve of that."

"No, and I don't think I have a bright future in arts writing." She tapped her finger to her chin. "Though I have learned a lot about Peruvian llama farming so far. Did you know that they were domesticated five thousand years ago?"

"Fascinating. Do you think that that'll sell the article?"

"Nope. So, tell you what," Amy said, "I'll trade you. One fact about me for a fact about you." She held up her hand in a scout salute. "No lies."

The clock on the wall ticked in silence. "And why would I be interested in facts about you?" Morgan asked.

"Because you've spent the entirety of these last few days staring at me like you want to open me up and see what's inside."

Amy held Morgan's gaze. Not many people could, but there was a hungry intensity in her expression. She had somehow put aside the stressed-out aura that she'd had yesterday, and now reminded Morgan of a cat stalking a bird. Her body language was deceptively soft as she sat sprawled in Morgan's comfy armchair, but her eyes sharp on her target.

Morgan snorted. "That's not true."

"Mm-hmm. How about this: three facts about me in exchange for one about you. That's a good exchange rate."

"I can ask you anything?"

"Anything."

"All right." Morgan tilted her head back and forth for a moment, as if trying to think of something, and then asked the question she'd hit upon a few days ago. "Did you change your name to that, or did your parents honestly give it to you?"

Amy's eyebrows rose, and then fell down into a vicious glare. Jackpot. "You looked me up."

"Of course I did. You're staying in my house. I had to make sure you weren't an axe murderer."

"You think Savannah would hire an axe murderer?"

"Savannah? No, but only because I think that if murder was on the agenda, she'd prefer to swing the axe herself."

Morgan pinned Amy with an expectant look, and let the silent seconds do their work as they ticked away.

"Fine," Amy said, and she looked genuinely embarrassed—not frustrated or irritated for once, but embarrassed. A faint tinge of blush crept over her cheekbones, setting off her few faint freckles. It was a good look on her.

"Yes," said Amethyst Sapphire Kelly, "my mom really did call me that. It could have been worse. I have a sister called Quartz Topaz."

Morgan chuckled. "You don't like being called Amethyst? That must be awkward at family get-togethers."

"No, but not that that matters. I don't do that sort of thing. I left town for good as soon as I could." Amy held up another finger. "And that was your second question."

"Well, hell." Morgan, distracted by her victory, was momentarily taken aback. "You got me there."

"Yup. So." Amy made a come-at-me-bro gesture, as cocky as a boxer. "One last question, whatever you want. Hit me. Dark secrets. Hidden agendas. Bra size."

Morgan pointed her fork at Amy. "What does your real smile look like?"

The expression in question faltered, but just for a moment. "What do you mean? I'm smiling right now."

"No you're not. I've met Savannah."

"And?"

"And that's her smile you're wearing."

Morgan popped a forkful of omelet into her mouth. What she was doing was a bastard move, sure—but it had been so long since she'd been able to be a bastard. You needed to be able to bring it to the table, sometimes to win in a boardroom. Since moving away, though, it had been muzzled and set aside, replaced by silence and awkwardness.

With some small surprise, she found that she'd honestly missed it.

"Quirk up the corners to show off the dimples," she continued, "but don't let it reach your eyes, so you don't get laughter lines. Lord forbid you wrinkle, after all. Tilt your head a little, just a bit to the side, just a little down. Everyone thinks that beauty requires symmetry, but a certain amount of crookedness is what's really charming." She finished her slice of toast. "You must have practiced it a lot, by the way. It's a winning copy."

Their gazes locked. Bit by bit, Amy's smile slipped away.

"Well, I don't feel like smiling right now, that's for sure."

Morgan looked at her expression. It was now steely instead of smiling, but at least it was Amy's actual expression, now, and not the copied reflection of a mentor on the opposite side of the planet.

"Maybe you should have been a reporter," Amy continued. "If you ever want to come back into the real world, I'm sure Savannah would hire you in a heartbeat."

"I don't think so," Morgan demurred, "for a variety of reasons." She raised her fork at Amy. "Well, there you go. You answered three questions, so now you get to ask one of your own. Shoot."

Amy paused, and gave her a sharp look across the coffee table.

Morgan waited patiently, ready for whatever the journalist might throw at her.

Would she repeat that pivotal question from her first interview: why did you leave? If she did, Morgan was ready to deflect it. She'd never been willing to talk about it at the best of times, and especially not now, after a morning spent with cute, perky Amy in her space, rummaging through her kitchen, filling the cottage with energy and light.

Used to being alone, it felt unnatural to Morgan.

"Where did you get all the dogs?"

Morgan blinked, and then cocked her head. "That wasn't what I was expecting you to ask."

Amy shrugged. "There are an awful lot of them. Anyone would be curious, wouldn't they?"

Okay, Amy could clearly read the waters, here; she'd steered away from the elephant in the room. Morgan leaned back, looking over the dogs, and couldn't stop a small smile from appearing. "I got them from the nearest animal shelter. Not all of them at once, I mean. I got them one after the other."

"Hah, yeah, I assumed as much. I think it'd raise a few eyebrows to walk into a shelter and be like," Amy spread her arms wide, "'give me all the dogs that you have!'"

"First it was Boris and Major. There was an article in the local newspaper, one of those 'last chance!' stories to tug readers' heartstrings. They both look intimidating, so they were on their last days. I didn't want to let that happen."

Amy came across as a prim and proper professional, used to the glamour of the big city. If Morgan had to picture her with a dog of her own, it would have been one something small and sweet, just the size to pop into a bag and take to a department store.

But on hearing Morgan's story, a flash of genuine sadness appeared in her eyes. Amy looked over at Major and Boris, crashed out in front of the fireplace in a tangle of long limbs. "Really? But they're so nice."

Morgan's heart beat harder. She ignored it and took another bite of her stolen omelet. "Well, apparently most people don't think so. When it came to wanting a family dog, they didn't picture these two blockheads."

At the hint of attention, the blockheads in question pricked up their ears and looked over. Morgan gestured for them to lie back down, and they did so, happy to go back to drinking in the heat of the fire.

"And then, well... after them, the same thing happened for Muffin—he needs regular shots, and no-one wanted to adopt a dog with medical issues—and O.J., too. His breed can have a bad reputation, but they're sweethearts."

"O.J.?" Amy's eyes twinkled. "That's not exactly what it says on his ID tag."

"The shelter named them," Morgan said, defensively. "That wasn't me."

"Mmm-hmm. I totally believe you."

Morgan ignored her and forged on. "And then when I was down there to sort out some paperwork, they were bringing in Bella. Her owner passed away; that's the only thing that I know about her past life. She's not exactly great with people, and the shelter was full to the gills with other, more adoptable dogs, so they had just made the decision to put her down."

Amy turned to look for the dog in question. Unlike the others, who liked to spend time up close and personal with humans, the little Maltese was nowhere in sight.

"She'll probably be in the bedroom," Morgan explained. "She likes her personal space."

"She's... different."

"She keeps to herself, mostly. I can't blame her."

"An antisocial loner, huh?" Amy pointedly didn't make eye contact with Morgan. "Sounds familiar. Hmm."

She looked out over the dogs, and then back to Morgan. Morgan assumed that she was going to keep talking about the dogs, but...

"It sounds like you must have been lonely."

"What?" Morgan raised an eyebrow. "No."

If Amy had just chased the why did you disappear? question like Morgan had expected, it would have been easy for Morgan to handle. She'd deflect and turn everything around, never answering anything clearly, until Amy got sick of asking and stormed off.

That would have been easy. Instead, Amy had asked something innocuous, and slowly, without even realizing it, Morgan had opened up to her.

Just a little.

But enough.

Morgan didn't like it.

"That's another question, and you only had one," Morgan said. She got to her feet, trying not to show regret at having to spitefully eat two omelets. "Okay, that's enough of this. I'm going to work on my projects. You should go and work on your article. I hear that the market for writing about llama farmers is a saturated one."

ele

Amy was... attractive.

It didn't cost Morgan anything to say that. She didn't even just mean physically, although that certainly was the case, too. Amy was enthusiastic about what she did, and tenacious—even if she was a little too easily rattled. Morgan had been able to get Amy to her breaking point several times over.

But... she was so familiar.

Not physically, of course. But that keen intent of the seasoned journalist, half friendly, half wanting to open you up and rummage through your organs, and that smile...

There was one principle that Morgan had stuck to in her professional life, and it was this: when you don't know what choice is the right one, don't just waver between them. Make the best choice that you can, and then roll up your sleeves and make it be the right choice through hard work and determination.

Three years ago, she'd made the choice to leave her old life behind. She'd committed to that, doing nothing by half measures.

How had it turned her into this person?

So this is what you gave up everything for? Amy had asked, and Morgan had agreed.

Morgan's new life was comfortable. It was quiet. No-one was close enough to her to expect anything of her, and she was free to do as she pleased. Just her, her art projects, and her dogs.

It was perfect.

But if it was so perfect, why did Amy's sudden appearance make her feel like someone had opened a window on a room that had been shut for too long?

Chapter Nine

Amy

In her cozy New Zealand home, Morgan Leithe has shed all remaining traces of the big-business tech mogul that she used to be.

No.

Despite the homely nest she's built for herself, Morgan Leithe is still the ruthless businesswoman who bought the tech industry to its knees.

No, that wasn't right, either.

Morgan Leithe cannot possibly eat two omelets, but if you get on her bad side, she'll do it just to punish you, because she's terrible.

Out on the back veranda, snuggled up under a rug with her laptop on her knees, Amy drummed her fingers against her keyboard and stared into the distance. Mount Ruapehu rose in the distance, imposing and icy.

Further along the outside of the cottage, the window of Morgan's forbidden art room opened onto the veranda to take in the same backdrop. Through it Amy could hear the sounds of her host, equally imposing and icy, doing whatever it was that she did in that room. Amy could hear the sound of the radio turned down low, and occasionally the vague sounds of things clinking and shuffling.

If she were a reader, what impression of Morgan would she get from Amy's attempts to capture her—at least, from the non-omelet related sentences?

Morgan was as easy to pin down as smoke. Sometimes she was cold and businesslike, out of place with her surroundings, but sometimes she looked like she'd been born in gumboots and worn woolen hats, impossible to imagine commanding a boardroom.

The woman was confusing, sometimes warm and friendly, sometimes cold; sometimes all business efficiency, sometimes awkward and stilted. How on earth was Amy supposed to explain her to a reader?

Amy closed her eyes and exhaled.

Morgan is 5'9" of cold calculating professionalism.

She also wears little woolen socks with kiwi birds knitted on them.

Sometimes when she thinks you're lying to her, she gives you a look like she can see right down into your soul and isn't impressed by what's in there, like there's nothing you could possibly hide from her.

She named one of her dogs Boris and another one Muffin.

She has a really nice mouth, when she's not scowling. And when she smiles, it's wider than you'd think...

Amy must have been daydreaming for a moment, because when she opened her eyes, there was a tennis ball in her lap that hadn't been there before. Amy broke out of her thoughts and looked down to see an expectant little dog face staring up at her, tail wagging.

Oh, why not? Amy picked up the ball for O.J.—ick, dog spit!—and threw it across the yard. The pitbull bounded off in hot pursuit, bouncing merrily in the snow in its little doggy snow booties.

She shook herself, looked back down to the document, and tried to bullshit herself out of her block. Scandinavians have known about the clarifying power of the cold for centuries. Perhaps Morgan's snow-change is the dip in the snow after the sauna, the perfect shock to the system. The question follows: what's next for this swdascvfgvdfbbbbbb

Oops. The ball was now back in her lap, after rolling across her keyboard. Sighing, Amy tossed it for O.J. again—wait, that was Muffin, that wasn't O.J...

Belatedly, as all the dogs began to swarm around their new play partner, assorted balls and toys in their mouths, Amy realized that she'd made a dire, dire mistake.

What could she do: not throw the balls for each and every one of them? Under the pressure of that many expectant little faces staring at her, it was impossible. She hurled them as fast as she could, a stream of happy dogs running back and forth to deposit them back in her lap, every lap leaving their treasured toys even more covered in dog drool and fur.

As the dogs' mom, Morgan could have called them off. Morgan, laughing audibly at Amy's predicament through the window of the art room, absolutely did not. Instead, she wandered outside to observe the ruckus. As Amy flailed, Morgan leaned back against the wall and wiped at her paint-covered hands with a rag. "Oh, good," she said. "They like you."

That wasn't entirely accurate. As usual, one of the dogs wasn't joining in. Looking unimpressed by the antics that were unfolding, Bella skulked at the edge of the veranda, keeping an eye on the rest of the pack, but holding her distance.

Amy pointed at the standoffish Maltese, her haughty attitude incongruous with her tiny mop body. "Uh, only mostly. Is there anything I can do to win her over?"

"Bella?" Morgan turned to look at her wayward doggy daughter, and her mouth creased in a smile. "Oh, she's fine. If she's sitting here watching you, she likes you, trust me. She's just not as playful as the others, but she's good comfort when you need it. Sometimes dogs are just like that." She chuckled. "People, too."

Are you like that? Amy wanted to ask—but she was prevented from asking such a sappy question by A) her good sense not to poke the bear when Morgan was finally smiling (even if what she was smiling at was Amy's misfortune), and B) the sudden appearance of Boris, lurching up on to her lap to try to press his spit-covered tennis ball right into Amy's face.

"Pflegh!"

"Okay, that's enough," Morgan said as Amy spluttered, and whistled. Like a well-trained army, the swarm wheeled on the spot and ran back to her. With a clearly practiced routine, Morgan efficiently stripped snow booties and jackets from her hounds and sent them back inside, somehow without getting more than a few stray hairs on her clothes.

It was dark magic, clearly. Amy chose to believe it was dark magic, and not the result of a clearly very sweet domestic routine, because if she thought too long about this billionaire ice queen laughing and playing with her dogs in the snow, then...

Amy turned her head back to the laptop, trying not to think about the way that she could feel her cheeks starting to heat. She raised her fingers to start to type again—and then paused, pulling a face. "Bleurgh," she said eloquently, and extended her hands, now thoroughly coated in dog slobber and fur, for Morgan to witness.

Morgan chuckled. "Yeah, that happens."

She tried to wipe it off, but that just made it worse. There was fur down her sleeves. There was fur in her hair. "Okay, I give up," Amy grumbled, and shut her laptop. "I think I need a shower."

Morgan paused. For a moment, it looked like she was wrestling with something. Then she straightened, some decision made. "Hmm. If you're done writing for now, I can do you one better than a shower," Morgan said, smiling wryly. "Trust me on this. Just give me a moment to set up."

Amy blinked. "Okay, sure."

Morgan headed out into the back yard, picking her way through the snow, and disappeared from view behind the garden shed. Five minutes later, during which Amy tried to rub her hands clean on her pants but instead just wound up making the whole situation at least fifty percent worse, Morgan re-emerged back into view.

She had an axe over one shoulder, like the most chic lumberjack in history. Amy swallowed hard.

"Okay, come here."

Amy made her way over, stepping in Morgan's boot prints to make the trek easier. "What, did you build me a cabin?"

"Even better." Morgan led her around the shed, then around behind a wooden screen, to—"Voila."

Hedged in behind the screen was a bathtub. Not just any bathtub: a thick old cast iron tub on clawed feet, deeper than the tiny apartment tub that Amy was used to. A small fire was burning underneath it, and steam was starting to rise in seductive coils from the surface. A clumsy little wooden shelf was placed next to the tub—another handmade item, Amy guessed—holding soap and shampoo and all the little niceties of life.

"There's some towels in the dryer right now, I'll bring you one when they're done," Morgan continued, as if she hadn't just casually revealed a setup that would make every cozy home blogger in America cry into their Instagram filters in jealousy. She gestured to the fire burning merrily away underneath the tub. "It's probably got half an hour's worth of good heat in it, then you'll need to put more wood on the fire."

"Half an hour's fine," Amy laughed, delighted. "I don't want to wrinkle up into a prune."

Morgan pulled her mouth to the side in a wry smile. "I have bad news for you about when you get to my age."

Amy scoffed. Sure, Morgan didn't look like a twenty-year-old anymore (Amy had dug up her college yearbook headshots—she knew it for sure), but for Morgan to act like she was over the hill was ridiculous, and Amy was going to let her know it. "Yeah, yeah. You just want to keep the whole silver fox look for yourself, I know how it is."

"Ha."

Morgan turned to leave Amy to it, but a suspicion had been forming in Amy's mind. "Hey," she said, before the other woman could leave. "You know, I'm beginning to think that you might actually be nice, under all of that glaring."

"Don't put that in the article," Morgan growled. "You'll ruin my reputation."

As Amy laughed, Morgan disappeared, leaving her to her own devices.

It took a moment for Amy to feel comfortable stripping off outside, but the little tub was boxed in by privacy screens, and the only high-rise neighbor around was Mount Ruapehu looming in the distance. Unless skiers in New Zealand were in the habit of taking military-level high-powered binoculars with them on the slopes, Amy was fairly sure that her privacy was secure.

She put her hair up in a loose bun and sunk down further under the water's surface. The air was full of the commingled scent of wood smoke and pine, and the goosebump-inducing bite of ice. The chill in the air nipped at every part of her that was above the water, but that just made it feel even better to sink further down into the hot water, feeling heat flush through her body.

The snow-capped mountain rose above Amy, icy clouds slowly shifting across its peak. But down in the water, listening to strange birdsong and the distant sound of Morgan talking to her dogs inside the house, Amy had never felt warmer.

Amy slung an arm out of the tub and rummaged in her clothes, slung over the nearby shelf. Fishing out her phone, she opened the camera, positioned it juuust so, and...

There. Cut just to show her legs in the water (carefully arranged so as to look their most appealing), steam rising from its surface, and then a backdrop of pine trees feeding up into a snow-covered mountain. The sun was just starting to streak the sky with oranges and pinks, and a constellation was already starting to show its twinkling face. No filter was needed when you were underneath a sunset like this.

Eat shit, Georgie, Amy thought with a smile on her face, and posted it.

What, they didn't let you use the bathroom inside the house? Georgie shot back, almost immediately. Poor thing.

Woah, Matias from work replied, looks pretty swanky!! what bed and breakfast is this??

Amy froze. Uh-oh, busted. Still, maybe New Zealand accommodation just normally came with elaborate Instagram-bait outdoor bathing setups! Matias had no reason to know otherwise, right? Maybe Amy would just ignore that particular reply and move on, and hope that no-one thought about it too much...

looks to me like she's got pretty cozy with a local, Olivia posted. ames, u dog.

Well, shit. Would anyone believe Amy if she said that she dropped her phone in the water at that exact moment, leaving her tragically unable to reply to Olivia's comment? Probably not, but the thought sure was tempting.

She replied with a dog emoji and a winky face, neither confirming nor denying anything, then set her phone to the side.

God, of course with her luck they'd got the wrong idea. Amy slid downward in the tub until her chin dipped into the water.

But, well... it may have been the wrong idea, but it was an enthralling one, wasn't it?

Morgan was a hot-and-cold pain in the ass, that was sure, giving Amy just enough to get her hopes up before yanking it away in one of her inexplicable moods... but she was still gorgeous.

Heat began to burn her cheeks at a particular thought.

No-one was around, right?

It was easy to imagine Morgan being as cold and forceful in bed as she was in the boardroom. But Amy didn't enjoy anything that seemed too easy, and that scenario was no different...

Instead, she let her eyes flutter shut and imagined the opposite. Morgan spread out on the bed, those icy eyes burning up at Amy in a mix of arousal and challenge, that wide mouth parting in a gasp just enough for a glimpse of tongue and teeth.

Try keeping your secrets now, she imagined herself whispering, and in her fantasies she slipped to her knees, Morgan's boyish hips held down between her hands. She pictured the feel of Morgan's skin under her mouth as she skated her lips, just barely touching her, down along the bared expanse of Morgan's stomach.

Don't tease, she imagined Morgan saying.

Me?, she'd say back. Never.

And then she pictured dropping lower...

Amy's hand slipped along her stomach and down between her legs, her knees trembling just a little where they jutted out of the water.

A flash of movement flickered in the corner of her vision. Amy yelped.

"There's that towel," Morgan said, as the offending object fluttered over the edge of the privacy screen. She paused. "Are you okay?"

"Yes!" Amy squeaked. "I'm fine! Thanks for the towel!"

When Morgan's footsteps retreated back into the house, Amy glared at Mount Ruapehu, as if ancient mountain formations could be threatened into submission. "This stays between you and me," she muttered, and then slipped downwards to dunk her head underneath the water, where no-one could see the way that her face was burning.

ele

All good things had to come to an end, and baths were unfortunately no exception to the rule. The water had begun to creep from pleasantly warm to very unpleasantly cold, the sky was darkening into gloom, and the little birds that were piping in the trees had long since closed up shop and headed back to their little birdy homes.

Farewell, best bathtime ever, Amy thought. With a heartfelt groan, she climbed out of the tub and toweled herself off, bare as the day she was born under the dimming sky.

This was such a gorgeous corner of the world. When she'd first rolled into town, she hadn't understood why Morgan, with all of the world at her fingertips, had decided to settle in the middle of nowhere.

Now, though... okay, Amy was definitely beginning to see the town's charms.

Maybe.

Just a little.

The wifi still sucked, though.

Her phone buzzed. Without thinking, Amy picked it up and flicked the screen on.

It was a new email from Savannah. It wasn't very long.

You haven't checked in recently. Don't slack off. Get me something juicy, or else.

Chapter Ten

Morgan

When Morgan had bought the little cottage, she'd instantly chosen this particular room to be her art room for the view of Mount Ruapehu out of its window. There was nothing like turning from a painting in progress, needing a break, and casting your eyes on a slice of nature like that. It was primal, the sort of thing that blew past all your mental shields to instantly recharge your artistic batteries.

Now, thought, her window was opening up to the view of the mountain —and, down in her yard, a view of the shed. It was growing dark, but from the other side of it, she could see the glow of the lights that she'd strung up for the tub.

Morgan gave up on her painting.

Having someone else around, even when she couldn't actually see them... it was distracting. It felt like having someone reading a book over her shoulder: even if she didn't mind what they were looking at, it still felt galling.

Too close. Too personal.

Amy being around was getting under her skin.

It wasn't bad. On paper, Amy had actually been the perfect houseguest. She hadn't done anything that Morgan could actually complain about: she hadn't let the dogs out, she hadn't cluttered the place up with trash or unwashed dishes, she hadn't broken the coffee machine.

Having someone just be around all the time, though, present in her house... it was just—strange.

Maudlin, and annoyed at herself for feeling so, Morgan left her studio and made her way over to the living room. It was time for a bottle of wine, a fire, and the rest of her novel.

As the lumber tycoon leveled his gun at Reuben Reid in the mill, Reuben thought fast. He tilted a saw blade, catching the light of the moon that was shining through a window, and reflected it forwards. In a heartbeat, the villain's gun dropped through his changing fingers, his body beginning to contort into the heinous shape— of a werewolf!

Morgan snorted. Of course the villain had been a secret werewolf. What an obvious twist.

The room was quiet save for the crackle of the fire, the snores of the dogs, and the sound of turning pages (Morgan wasn't entirely sold on the idea that pushing someone into a running sawmill counted as defeating them in ritual werewolf combat, but according to werewolf law, Reuben was now apparently the leader of a brand new pack).

Eventually, though, Morgan heard the sound of Amy making her way back inside through the snow and up to the veranda door, grumbling under her breath and letting out little brr! noises. Morgan chuckled to herself. Getting warm and toasty in the outside bath felt like a godsend in chilly weather, but after you got out, everything felt twice as cold.

Amy stepped inside and shut the door behind her, shivering loudly.

Morgan looked up from her book. "You liked it?"

"Whew! Snow aside, it was perfect." Amy tucked a still-damp curl behind an ear. "I'm going to go with a new angle: forget your old life, Morgan Leithe, here comes your new career as a B&B host."

"You couldn't pay me enough to have people in my house all the time."

Amy laughed. "I'm the same way. I think I'd go crazy if I had to have people around, even if they were paying a slice of my rent."

"Ha." Morgan hesitated, caught on the cusp of a decision...

Amy had been nice to her that morning. It had taken Morgan a little while to realize it: having someone stomping around her house and messing up all of her stuff didn't seem like being nice to her—but to a normal person, someone helping you with breakfast and then playing with your dogs was nice, wasn't it?

And in response, she'd been a real witch. Even if she'd never apologize in words, the bath had been a nice peace offering.

Now, she could keep going on the way she'd been doing so, treating Amy like an enemy... or she could swallow her feelings of awkwardness and try to bridge the gap between them, negotiating some kind of peace.

No, scrap that. That sounded too much like merger talk. This wasn't all business, no matter the interview hanging between them—this was a young woman who'd had the rotten luck to get stuck with the crankiest ice queen this side of Mount Ruapehu.

An attractive young woman...

Morgan sighed at herself, and nipped that particular thought right in the bud. She gestured towards the couch. "Come here. Sit. Fill me in on what's been happening in the real world."

"Like what?" Amy's eyes narrowed a touch, clearly suspicious.

Morgan held up a hand in pacification. "Nothing personal. Just like... is the CEO of VirtualTech still trying to push augmented reality glasses as the future of phone design?"

"Oh, god." Amy rolled her eyes, and then sat down next to her. "You really haven't heard? No, he's moved on to the next big thing: neural implants. Right into the brain. He doesn't have a single neurologist on staff, but he's head-hunting every design and marketing guru that he can get his hot little hands on. Priorities, right?"

Over the next while, Amy filled Morgan in on the ins and outs of the tech scene over the past few years. Morgan listened, scoffing at the tales of new disasters, humming appreciatively at the news of creative innovations. "You know a lot about the industry," she said, after a while.

Amy shrugged. "I needed to pick it up quickly. It's my job, after all."

"You weren't into technology before joining Zero Nova?"

Amy shook her head. "Nope. But there was a job opening for a junior reporter, and it wasn't demanding that applicants had seven years of experience, four award-winning exposes, and a personal recommendation from Anderson Cooper already under their belts—it didn't matter what subject the magazine was about." She laughed. "If it had turned out to be about lawn care, then right now I'd be trying to get the hot goss on turf care out of you."

That was the sort of moxy that Morgan had liked to see in her own employees. "So what got you into it, if not the material? People don't tend to accidentally become journalists."

Amy gave her a subdued little smile, just barely quirking the corner of her mouth upward. "I just liked... finding things out. Sharing information. Telling stories." She looked down into her wine glass. "Well, it didn't immediately seem like there were all that many stories in tech writing, starting out. It just looked like specs and release dates, you know? But taking a lot of facts and trying to come up with the best way to share them with people—the shortest, sharpest, slickest way, catching their attention and making them go 'ooh'—that's fun! It's like a little puzzle. I enjoy it."

"Some people just do sudokus."

Amy laughed. "Sudokus don't make for a five year plan. Well, maybe they do. I never manage to get past filling in all the threes." Then she caught Morgan looking at her strangely, and tilted her head. "What? Something on my face?"

"No, nothing," Morgan said, and took a sip of her wine to cover the moment of her hesitation. "Just thinking about sudokus."

There is it, she thought to herself. That's your real smile.

Laughing over her own stupid joke, Amy had unwound a little. That carefully-rehearsed reporter smile, handed down from Savannah, had disappeared—and it turned out that underneath it was a bright, goofy grin.

Amy gave her a wry look, as if she could see the words that Morgan hadn't said. "Well, okay." She laced her fingers together and cracked her knuckles. "So, I wasn't kidding this morning. Do you have any board games around here?"

Amy's phone dinged. Without reading the message she'd just received, Amy turned it to silent.

"Not anything important?"

"No." Amy smiled brightly. "Or, at least, it's not something that I want to deal with right now. So: are you a Scrabble person, or a Monopoly person?"

Chapter Eleven

Amy

The problem with snow, Amy decided, was that it looked pristine and beautiful to the naked eye, but it was a bitch to take a selfie in.

She tried yet again, tilting her face to get her good angle, holding her camera just so, trying to capture the gorgeous winter landscape behind her, fluffy marshmallow clouds and fat falling snowflakes and the looming presence of Mount Ruapehu...

...And for her troubles, she got yet another snap with a terrible white balance, her face washed out and the backdrop reduced to an unimpressive white blur.

For all that anyone could tell, she could have been trapped in a walk-in freezer. Not a good look.

What was the point of being in a gorgeous location if you couldn't even rub it in your frenemy's face properly? Ugh. Giving up, Amy slapped a filter on it and pressed send.

A string of reaction notifications popped up. Ooomg, jealous!, Matias replied.

Within a minute, Georgie had tagged her in a photo right back. Amy opened it to find a shot of Georgie on a deckchair, pristine sand beneath her, cocktail in one hand and her laptop balanced on her tanned legs as she lounged in her expensive bathing suit... and on the laptop's screen, highlighted with emojis so that Amy absolutely couldn't miss it, a word count that was significantly higher than her own.

Amy scowled. Taut, tanned thighs she could care less about—but a higher word count? Disgusting.

Amy sat down with a world-weary groan on the veranda armchair, swiping to refresh her feed. Another few reactions trickled in, and then stopped. She swiped again, but that was apparently that.

She sighed, leaning back against the overstuffed chair, and kicked her feet idly against the wooden boards.

Despite having lived in the town for years, Morgan hadn't made any close friends. She was cut off from the locals, floating all on her own, only communicating when she absolutely needed to.

Amy had thought that it was sad, honestly. Tragic, even.

Now, her thumb automatically swiping on its own to see if any more notifications would pop up, Amy wondered if she really had any room to judge. Her list of friends on social media was sizable, sure, but what did that really mean for her? Was getting a handful of comments and reaction emojis on a post really all that different to giving someone a polite nod in the street and then moving on?

Was she just as alone as Morgan...?

Ugh! She drew her gloved hands down her face, groaning. All this snow was making her maudlin. It was probably, like, a hormonal thing. She'd been plunged from a blazing hot New York summer straight into the icy depths of a New Zealand winter—that had to be what was messing with her. She probably needed some vitamin C, or something like that.

That was it, Amy decided, and got up from her seat. She'd eat an orange, and then everything would be fine. She didn't need social media. She didn't need vague acquaintances. Notifications, likes, follows? Who needed them?! Not her!

Her phone buzzed. She sat back down and unlocked it again.

anyone got an ark?? Marie posted, followed by a string of crying emojis. Underneath it was a photo of the Bellbird Cafe—now in a much more miserable state than when Amy had seen it last. The roof was leaking, and instead of the slow drip that Amy had seen last, it was several vigorous leaks. One of the photos was of water leaking out from inside a power point, which... okay, Amy wasn't a certified electrician, but she was pretty sure that that wasn't good.

we're shutting down until jerry g can make it over and work his magic, Marie posted, with an even longer chain of crying emojis. so everyone come take all this bacon and milk off our hands before they go to waste!!!

Amy had been tagged, along with what looked like half of the town. She looked at the post as she wandered inside to get another cup of coffee.

"Who's Jerry?" Amy asked.

"Hmm?" Morgan, reading a book on the couch, didn't look up. "Oh, Jerry Gordon? He's the local electrician, lives a town over."

Ah-ha, the post made more sense. "So he can't get over here until the snow lifts? Okay, I see."

Morgan finally looked up from her coffee. "Is there something you need fixed?"

Something in her eyes made Amy's mouth quirk into a smile. Was that a spark of eagerness in the ice queen's gaze? Just a tiny one?

Amy tapped her phone to her lips, hiding her smile. "You were an engineer, weren't you?" she asked, as if she didn't have Morgan's entire life history committed to memory.

"More computers than heavy machinery, but I can do a little bit of everything," Morgan agreed, and then, to Amy's joy, followed that with "I haven't got my hands dirty in a long time, but I still know my way around a circuit breaker. I'm not busy right now, if there's an issue."

"Excellent," Amy said with a grin, and started typing on her phone. "I'll let Marie know you'll be over in a little while."

Morgan looked at Amy like she'd grown a second head. "Pardon?"

Amy turned her phone around to show Morgan the status update. "You didn't hear?"

Morgan now looked like Amy had grown a third head, and all three of them were speaking gibberish. The edge of eagerness that Amy had thought she'd seen earlier had scampered for the hills, and instead in its place was a hint of panic. "I don't... I don't keep track of what goes on. I'm not exactly close with Marie."

You're not exactly close with ANYONE here, Amy thought—but it had been nearly 24 hours since Morgan had had one of her icy snaps, so she kept that particular thought to herself.

They hadn't become bosom buddies or anything. They'd played a few games of Scrabble, working their way through some nice wine, and then called it a night.

Still, it was a side of Morgan that Amy was keen to keep seeing more of —even if she had utterly trounced Amy in with quixotic on a triple.

Amy looked back down at her phone, and tapped away at a reply. "Well, they're having a problem with the electrics over at the Bellbird, and you're just the superhero they need!" She hit send. "I told Marie you'd be over in a bit. Off you go, wonder woman."

"Knock that off," Morgan groused. She scowled, but there was something uncertain about it. "Marie said she wants me over?"

"Well, no, I volunteered you." Amy's phone buzzed in her hand, and she looked down again. "But—there we go, she says she'll be expecting you."

Morgan drummed her fingers on the table, and for a moment Amy was sure that she'd refuse... but then she sighed and got to her feet. "That roof's been leaking for a while, but it shouldn't take too long to seal it... and I guess if it's just a matter of getting out a multimeter and checking the electrics, then, well... it'll be days before Jerry can get over here, after all..."

Watching Morgan slip into business mode was something else for sure. Amy watched in wide-eyed delight as the other woman's face seemed to hone in on a sharper focus, clearly assessing the small-town problem like it was a billion-dollar multinational project.

Muttering to herself about tools and power and god knows what, Morgan slipped on a jacket and her boots. "This shouldn't take long," she said, putting on her gloves. "Two hours, maybe. Three, if it's as bad as the rest of the wiring in this town. The dogs have had their breakfasts, don't let them convince you that they haven't."

"I think I can stand up to a pack of mutts," Amy said, despite all the evidence she'd displayed to the contrary. She flapped her hands in a go, shoo gesture. "Bring home some bacon."

Morgan rolled her eyes, and then she was gone, banging the door closed in its warping doorframe a couple of times until it finally stayed shut. And then it was just Amy—and a pack of dogs who were acting like they hadn't been fed in weeks—left alone in the house.

The proper thing to do would have been to go back to her shambles of an article and to try to squeeze yet more blood from that stone.

The thing she really, really wanted to do was to go back to the guest room, snuggle down under a knitted blanket, and learn more about llamas. Maybe the snowstorm would never end, and she'd never have to go back to work. Maybe it could just be her, a pack of friendly mutts, and getting her ass kicked by a billionaire at Scrabble, snowed in for eternity.

It wasn't the worst thought. But she'd put off Savannah's last email as long as she could, and daydreaming about being a live-in Scrabble submissive was just procrastination.

Amy knew what she had to do—it was the whole reason she'd been sent half-way around the world in the first place, wasn't it?

If this opportunity had come a week earlier, it would have struck Amy as exciting. Sneaking around in an ex-billionaire's house! Finding secrets!

...But now, after getting to know the other woman a little, something about what Amy was doing stuck in her throat.

Focus, Amy, she warned herself. Eyes on the prize.

She closed her eyes, took a deep breath, and then opened them again.

Now, if I were an eccentric billionaire, where would I hide my juiciest secrets?

It wasn't exactly the sort of thing that you were taught in school. Amy wandered from room to room, the pack of dogs following in her footsteps just in case she was about to do anything interesting.

Sorry for spying, little guys! she thought as they followed at her heels, tails wagging eagerly. Please don't tell your mom!

The obvious contender for a shakedown was Morgan's computer. Amy paused in the living room, eyeing the battered, sturdy laptop on the coffee table. But Morgan was, after all, a tech genius—she'd have security measures, surely. Keyloggers, passwords, that kind of thing. Amy knew her way around the basics of IT, but she also knew that she'd be well and truly outclassed in this arena.

And even if she somehow wasn't... What if Morgan came home unexpectedly? How fast could Amy shut down everything and make the laptop look like it hadn't been messed with? Longer than it would take for Morgan to walk down the hallway, Amy was sure.

Amy bit the inside of her cheek at the thought of being caught in the act. No ma'am, she did not want that to happen. The computer was off the table.

Where else to look? Amy continued wandering through the house. The veranda? Not likely to be many secrets there. The kitchen? Probably no secrets there (unless you included the way that Morgan had cute oven mitts with ducks on them). The bookshelves? The only secret there was how Morgan managed to stand those god awful vampire detective novels.

Should she rummage through Morgan's bedroom drawers, like a thief in a movie? Amy didn't know what would be in there, but that was what they always did in TV shows, right? She could see the thrilling headlines already: breaking news! mysterious and reclusive tech genius has some naughty underwear at the back of her panty drawer! The world wouldn't exactly catch ablaze with that piece of information

A silly little smile formed on Amy's lips. A stupid headline, true. Not helpful right now, true. Tempting to picture? Also true.

Bathroom? No. Laundry room? Probably not. The art room...

Amy paused outside the ever-closed door of Morgan's art room.

It was the whole Bluebeard thing, right? When a mysterious person told you not to do one specific thing... well, who could resist doing that exact thing? Eve hadn't, the latest Mrs. Bluebeard hadn't, and Amy, desperate for any delicious morsel of info to report back to her boss, certainly couldn't hold herself back.

The door wasn't locked. Despite knowing that she was alone in the house, Amy opened the door as quietly as she could, the door squeaking a little in protest.

Inside the top secret forbidden art room was... art?

It was what she'd expected, but it still took her by surprise. Amy's eyes grew wide as she took in the sight of the room.

Piles of reference books were stacked around the room in messy heaps, dog-eared and well-thumbed-through. A drafter's chair, its leather comfortably worn, sat in front of an easel, next to an overflowing pile of brushes and pencils, paper scraps and paint-tubes, everything an artist could need within arm's length.

And around the walls... Amy rushed forward despite herself, needing to see more. They were mostly sketches, charcoal lines and pencil picking out graceful figures. Artistic figures and landscapes, mostly, magazine photos for reference pinned up next to them, and—Amy let out a little laugh—some drawings of Morgan's dogs, their mouths open in happy smiles as their owner captured them in quick, loose gesture sketches.

Amy had Morgan's entire life pinned down in her dossier, but she'd never once managed to get a glimpse of this side of her! But the proof was here, in every aspect of the cozy little room, the perfect little artist's nest.

She remembered Morgan asking her What do you do for a hobby? No wonder that the older woman had looked a little at a loss when Amy confessed to not having one. This was clearly something that bought Morgan a lot of joy.

There was a bottle of wine on the table—the second one that Amy had shared with Morgan yesterday. Morgan must have taken it in here after Amy had retreated off to bed, mourning her losses.

Amy picked it up and gave it a little heft, testing its weight. And Morgan had spent a while in here with it, too, because it had gone from mostly-full to empty overnight.

That almost sounded like some real detective work! Good job, Ames!

Growing bolder, Amy sat down in Morgan's chair, giving it a little swivel from side to side to see how it felt. Morgan must have been sitting here, with the bottle of wine to her side. It felt strangely intimate to slip into her spot. The easel in front of her was empty, and the paintbrushes were all dry; Amy was pretty sure that the older woman hadn't been painting. What else did the great Morgan Leithe like to do when she was drinking?

Underneath the easel, there was a notebook on the floor, spine up and pages open, as if it had been dropped. Amy picked it up absent-mindedly.

This particular notebook was dated in Morgan's military-neat handwriting as being from a few years ago. And inside were... more life-drawing figures?

Amy paged through the sketch-covered pages. Morgan really had a favorite theme. She was good at what she did, though, shadow and line coming together to give weight to the figures, to make them look real. In all of her years, Amy had never managed to draw more than stick figures, but she could tell when a drawing looked impressive.

She flipped through the pages. A model, gathered fabric held at her side to fall in complex folds... a twisting nude torso, muscle sleeting down her shoulders to tug at her lower back as she turned, all in graceful lines... another nude model, lying down languidly with her hands stretched below her stomach to touch—

Amy dropped the book.

Um.

Okay, that one had been a little more than a regular nude model. Like, Amy had never been to an art class before, but she was pretty sure that they didn't ask the life-drawing models to do that!

Or if they did, then she definitely needed to grab a pencil and notebook and sign up for a class some time. Yowza.

For a while, she sat there and turned through the pages, eyes wide.

As she did, two things became clear.

The first thing was that Morgan hadn't been drawing in an art class— these women, coy and rapturous by turns, were clearly in bed with the artist, their eyes burning with need at the artist as they were pinned down on the paper.

The second thing that this meant, both obvious and mind-blowing at the same time, was that Morgan was into women.

Like any lesbian worth her salt, Amy was used to wishing that all her favorite unobtainable hot women were into women.

Celebrity actresses that she'd never met in her life? Definitely secretly gay.

Her tragically-straight college crushes? One day she'd open Facebook to see their tearful reveals about how they were getting divorced from their boring husbands and starting over in their new lives as sexy butch welders.

The hot woman who was always ahead of her in the line at her regular morning Starbucks run? Secretly burning with the forbidden wish to turn and ask a certain journalist for her number, overcome with lust by the mere mention of almond milk flat whites.

Morgan Leithe, with her laser death glare and her diamond-cut cheekbones? Amy's brain hadn't hesitated to provide her with fantasies. It was all a silly little fun daydream.

But to find out that she was right? That was unimaginable. She had to take a moment to stare into space, letting that filter into her mind.

Morgan, into women. Morgan: into women? Morgan... into... women!

In a daze, Amy kept turning the pages.

More women looked up at her from under their lashes, or didn't look at all, their eyes shut as their bodies writhed, flesh expertly rendered. It wasn't the artistic skill with shading that was making Amy's face flush hot enough to hurt, though.

When Amy, gawping, was finally able to turn her attention away from some very particular details up to the drawn faces, a revelation slapped her in the face.

These weren't different women.

They were all the same woman.

And Amy knew her.

She had a different hairstyle—and, more importantly, Amy had never seen her boss naked before—but this was unmistakably Savannah. Amy would recognize those bright, sharp eyes and that crooked little fox-like smile anywhere.

Here, Morgan had captured Savannah from the side, looking over her shoulder at Morgan, mouth quirked in a smile. Here, Savannah stared defiantly at her artist, shoulders and thighs held in place with beautiful, intricately-knotted ropes. In another, she was smiling down off of the page, her hair mussed and her defenses down in a tender moment.

The rest of the pages were free from random nude models—this notebook had started with art models, but the rest of the pages were of Savannah, Savannah, Savannah.

What was going on?!

Chapter Twelve

Morgan

"Morgan."

"Marie."

"Amy said you were coming over to fix this." Marie looked suspicious. "I didn't believe that she could crowbar you out of your hidey-hole, honestly."

"You're welcome," Morgan said, dryly.

The two of them stood behind the Bellbird's bar. In the dining area, townspeople came and went, chatting and laughing in the gloom of the unlit room as Kaia parceled out all the kitchen goodies that were languishing, unrefrigerated.

"Milk? Do I have a taker for milk? I have almond, soy, and regular ol' cow..."

"Butter, butter, come get your butter!"

"Oh no, the good bacon... I was looking forward to that! Oh well, our fridge at home is full full, better that it doesn't go to waste..."

Marie looked over the dark kitchen, all its lights and heating turned off. "Can you really fix this sort of thing?"

Morgan fought the urge to roll her eyes. "Or your money back."

It was going to be easy. It may have been a long time since Morgan had really got her hands dirty with electrical work, but that didn't mean that she'd forgotten everything that she'd ever picked up. She'd get up into the roof space, do her thing, and then she'd be able to flee back to the safety of her house.

Well, the relative safety, anyway. She'd thought that she'd been safe from social interactions when she was in the privacy of her own damned living room, but Amy had certainly destroyed that illusion.

Still, it's not like there was much small-chat that she'd have to do up in the roof. At least that wasn't going to be awkward—

"Hey, everyone! Morgan's gonna fix the electricity!"

Everyone in the Bellbird turned to look at Morgan. Morgan turned to look at Kaia.

"What?" said Kaia. "Don't worry, I'll save you some bacon and eggs."

"Are you an electrician?" That was... Morgan knew her face, but she didn't know her name. The woman who ran the visitor's center.

"I don't have the proper certifications in this country, but I can fix a few things," Morgan said, trying to dodge the question—and, more importantly, the attention.

Someone else that Morgan recognized from the local grocery store laughed. "Hell, I should have called you to wire up my shed. Your call-out rates have gotta be lower than Jerry's."

Morgan had commanded deals worth billions of dollars. Now, though, with the townspeople looking at her like she was a particularly curious zoo exhibit, she felt just like she had in her first years at her start-up again, giving her first speeches to potential investors. She felt like she should have been about to begin a Powerpoint presentation.

Help came from an unlikely ally. "All right, people," Marie started, clapping her hands. "We don't have all day. Get that bacon moving."

Morgan took her opening. "I'm just going to get into it," she said, and tilted her chin towards the ceiling. "Is there a ladder around?"

Five minutes later she was upside-down in the roof space, blowing cobwebs away from her face, lying in a puddle of leaking water.

With some surprise, she realized that she'd missed this sort of thing.

Morgan handed her flashlight down to Kaia, perched on the ladder. "Could you hold it—great, yes, right there."

Kaia squinted, and then pointed. "That light switch, and that power point there, they were both dripping water. I'm no techie, but I was like, 'well, that's probably not good.'"

"Yeah, I can see the problem." Morgan kept her eye on the hole, making mental notes of the patch-job it needed. "It looks alarming, but it's really not that big of a deal. Once I fix the leak and everything dries off, it should all be back to working order."

"Wow, a woman of many talents. I never knew."

Morgan shrugged as much as she could in her position. "It's good to maintain a little bit of mystery."

"There's a little bit of mystery and then there's, like, secret-Russian-spy levels of mystery." Kaia laughed a little, but it wasn't unkind.

It didn't take Morgan long to patch the leaks. After that, everything just needed to dry off. She slid down the ladder back into the cafe. "All done."

Marie tilted her head. "Well, that didn't take long."

"It looked worse than it actually was," Morgan explained, wiping the grime off of her hands. "Most things like this do."

"Hmm," Marie said, noncommittally.

Kaia elbowed her mom.

Marie frowned at the silent kitchen. "I can't make coffees without power, but... cordial?"

In a few minutes' time, Morgan found herself having a drink with two people she'd never exchanged more than a few words with.

Internally, she wanted nothing more than to run back to her cottage, returning to her own little world.

But... Amy would find out. People liked talking to Amy, and vice-versa. For some reason, the thought of looking foolish in front of Amy made her feel... uncomfortable.

She fought the urge to squirm.

Kaia took pity on her. She gave Morgan a grin. If she really was Marie's daughter, she was doing a good job of hiding it, that was for sure. "I never knew you could do this sort of thing. You've been keeping secrets from us all." She tapped her phone. "Add me on Facebook?"

Morgan hesitated, and then shook her head. "I don't do that."

"Social media? C'mon, it's not that hard, you should make a profile."

Morgan frowned. "It's... not really for me."

Anyone with social graces might have dropped the topic at that. Unluckily for Morgan, however, New Zealanders weren't exactly into that kind of thing. At first, Morgan had thought that their friendly bluntness was charming; now that she was on the receiving end of it, however, her opinion was changing somewhat.

Kaia cocked her head to the side. "Yeah? Why not?"

It was something that Morgan had never broached with anyone in town. What was she going to do: swan into town saying Hello, nice to meet you all, I'm actually a big deal, and hand out Non-Disclosure Agreements for everyone to sign?

And yet... as far as she knew, no-one had leaked her info. She'd been braced for it, ready to pull up her roots and find a new little town to settle down in when this one was ruined for her, but the onslaught of media attention had never eventuated.

Well, until Amy, anyway. And Amy couldn't be blamed on the townspeople.

"I... don't exactly want people to find me."

Kaia and Marie looked at each other. "Yeah, the whole celebrity thing? We figured as much. I think Jocelyn's son, you know the one who lives down Wellington? He saw you when he was in town visiting his mum. He's into all that tech stuff. Loves his phones and all. But mum told him to keep it hush-hush."

Morgan stared. "She did?"

Marie didn't turn to look at her. Kaia continued with a laugh. "Yeah, and, like... it's kind of cool, honestly? I mean, having our very own secret billionaire around."

"We get them all the time," Marie said, shooting daggers at her daughter. "Rich tourists who just use the town as their playground, and then leave for the next adventure." She crossed her arms, staring Morgan down. "We may be a tourist destination, but we're still a community."

"Mum, jeez!" Kaia rolled her eyes. "C'mon," she continued, pointing at Morgan's phone. "Just make a fake one. When I was working a boring stiff job I didn't want my boss to see what I got up to in my free time, so that's what I did."

Under this torrent of friendly pressure, Morgan had no choice. She got her phone out with a sigh, and opened it up. Here goes nothing.

A fake profile, huh...? Morgan wracked her brain for a fake name, and then punched in the first one that came to mind. Kaia didn't need to know that it was the name of a secret immortal assassin from the Reuben Reid books.

"Look," Kaia continued, delighted, "now add your interests."

Morgan punched in STEM NGOs, renewable energy, and community-based solutions.

Kaia dropped her chin into her hand. "Okay, well, I have 'the Simpsons' and 'dogs' in mine, but you do you."

Marie was less polite. "No, come on," she said, giving up the presence that she hadn't been snooping over Morgan's shoulder. "You have to have something less... less..."

"Pretentious?"

"I was gonna go with boring, but you said it, not me. Anyway," she huffed, walking away and back around the counter, "this is you being undercover, right? You don't want to put your big important interests in it."

Morgan hesitated, her thumbs hovering over the keyboard. After a moment, she backspaced all of that, and slowly typed in...

Kaia laughed. "Oh god, another person into bloody Reuben Reid."

Marie's head turned. She stared at Morgan. "You like the Reuben Reid books?"

Morgan stared back at her. "Yes."

"Mum likes those books too! Loves them, in fact." Kaia laughed. "Why haven't you two figured this out before now? You could've been running a little book club."

The electrics in the cafe had been fixed, but Marie looked like she was about to pop a fuse of her own. She flapped her hands at her daughter, like she was shooing away seagulls. "Shoosh, you." Marie looked at Morgan, as guarded and neutral as any corporate negotiator. "Well, what did you think of the new one?"

Marie wanted to talk. Here was a chance for Morgan to act like a real human instead of a strange loner. The polite thing to do would have been to keep the conversation pleasant.

She was tired, she was damp, and she was feeling wrung-out from unexpectedly social interactions. Fake politeness was beyond her. "I thought the ending was a cop-out," she said instead, knowing that she was being rude even as it was coming out of her mouth. "The villain was the long-lost head of the Blackfang pack?" She shook her head. "Someone wanted a sequel and didn't care if it was forced."

There was a moment of tense silence, and then...

"Ha!" Marie grinned. "I thought the same. Though it was good that he finally got together with Ayverigh."

"Now, I can't follow you there," Morgan said. "He has much better tension with Ryghlee."

"Oh, you would think something like that," Marie said, and Morgan had no idea what that was supposed to mean, but when the other woman said it, she was smiling.

Just a little, mind.

But that was progress.

A while later, after Morgan's taste in Reuben Reid characters had been thoroughly savaged—Morgan had got her own back by suggesting that the sudden appearance of the fae at the end of book 12 had been a deeply stupid plot twist, making Marie fume—and all the cordial had been finished, Kaia walked Morgan out of the Bellbird.

"Thanks again for the help. I know mum can get cranky, but she appreciated it." Kaia cocked her head, looking up at Morgan. "You know, you've been here a few years, but I don't think we've ever had an actual conversation."

"I'm not exactly talkative," Morgan said. She put her hands in her pockets.

"Believe me, I noticed." Kaia looked down at her phone, and then finished what she was doing. "Okay, I've friended you," she said. "So now if you need anything, you can message me."

"Sure."

She looked sideways at Morgan from the corner of her eyes. "Or, like, if you want to grab a coffee or something sometime... maybe not in Mum's cafe though, that'd be kind of awkward, ha."

"Sure—wait, what?"

Kaia shrugged, still grinning. "Or tea? Wine? Beer? I don't know what you like, but I'd like to find out."

Morgan stared. "Kaia, are you... asking me out?"

It was blunt, but after everything that had gone on that day, Morgan was long past the ability to be subtle.

Happily, though, New Zealanders seemed to appreciate a blunt approach more than Americans. Kaia was no exception. "Yeah!" The younger woman, usually a beam of sunshine, suddenly looked a little apologetic. "Sorry, is my gaydar wrong? It's usually pretty spot-on."

Morgan let out a breath. "No, you're right."

"Yesss." Kaia fist-pumped. "Go team massive lesbian. So... want to get a drink, sometime?"

It had been so long since Morgan had been with a woman.

Kaia was fun. She was attractive. She made delicious strawberry jam.

But... Morgan didn't want her.

Because... because...

Because Morgan wanted someone else.

The recognition hit her hard, and then it seemed to rise like carbonation, filling her mind with dizzying bubbles.

She'd sworn to never love again. She'd fled to the opposite side of the globe and locked her heart away like a princess in an old fairy-tale, telling herself that it was safer that way.

It had hunted her down regardless.

What it was wasn't love—Morgan knew that. She'd only known Amy for a few days, and love was something that needed time to grow and flourish, reaching its roots deep into you.

But as she looked at Kaia, Morgan couldn't imagine pulling her into her arms—not because of anything that Kaia lacked, but because when she imagined holding someone close, Amy was the only person that came to mind. Someone who had got deep under her skin without Morgan even realizing it.

"I—"

Despite Morgan's complete lack of eloquence, Kaia seemed to recognize what was up. "Ah, don't worry about it." Kaia gave her a little rueful grin. "I just thought I'd try my luck. The gay dating scene isn't exactly booming all the way out here. No hard feelings. I guess you and that American girl...?

Morgan's heart rate spiked, like she'd been caught out in a terrible secret. "Amy? No, she's just in town to interview me. We barely know each other."

"Oh, really?" Kaia was taken aback. She looked out of the corner of her eyes at Morgan, thoughtful. "Huh. Shows what I know, I guess."

With a small smile, Kaia put her phone back in her pocket, then gave Morgan a wave. "Catch you later, Morgan. Bring Amy around, sometime."

Chapter Thirteen

Amy

One long, hot shower later, mostly spent staring blankly at the walls, Amy came to the decision that she needed to avoid Morgan.

Avoiding the other woman was the opposite of her job description- and, right now, the opposite of what she really, really wanted to do—but she couldn't risk it.

She was one big confused mess. She needed a moment to sort herself out, unless she wanted to run the risk of blurting out so, hey, quick question, or, actually, you know, more of an observation, really: you used to fuck my boss?

Morgan was a cold-hearted business genius. Morgan was an awkward dog-mom in woolen socks. Morgan was a secret sex goddess, with Amy's boss tied up and waiting for her.

Amy couldn't let slip that she'd seen what she'd seen. This secret stolen information was... unbelievable. She had no idea what to think about it. Once she'd cooled down a little, and put her professional persona back on... then she'd be fine, she reasoned.

Amy could play it cool until she found out what the hell was going on.

Maybe. Probably.

Flushed in a way that had nothing to do with the heat of her shower, Amy slipped on her borrowed snow gear and headed out to the Red Deer Lodge. Going out for a bite! she wrote on a post-in note, and didn't add so I can avoid you until I can stop thinking about your secret sex life!

One short walk later, Amy had made her escape. When she stepped into the warmth of the cozy little restaurant, someone called her name. Her gaze snapped up... and found the three backpackers, crowded around the bar in a raucous knot of locals.

"Amy!" Will yelled. He jostled the people next to him, clearing a space for her, and gave the bar a pat. "Come have a drink! It's my birthday!"

"Happy birthday!" Amy chimed, but her eyes darted around the bar.

There was no sight of Morgan.

Despite the fact that her plan was to avoid Morgan, some part of her felt almost disappointed.

"Mate, you look down." Natalie slung an arm around Amy. "Want to talk about it?"

Absolutely not. "The next round's on me!" she said by way of distraction, to a round of cheers. Then, as the beers began to arrive, she squared her shoulders. "Aussies like to drink, right? Show me a drinking game."

Natalie and James laughed, and Will placed his hand over his heart. "Mate, I have never heard a more welcome request."

Drinks in exotic locales on the company dime—what could be better? It was exactly the sort of thing that she'd dreamed of as a baby journalist, sneaking longing looks at the senior reporters' travel accounts. One day, she'd sworn, that would be her.

And, well, to be honest: it was pretty freaking great.

But right at that moment... it wasn't what she wanted.

Somewhere after being shown the intricacies of a game called Two-Up, which she was beginning to suspect was actually a joke they were playing on her, and learning how to chant the traditional song of Aussie Aussie Aussie Oi Oi Oi—a drinking song made of nothing but two words, and therefore perfect for extremely drunk people—Amy found herself in a quiet little bubble in the conversation.

It was one of those little spaces you sometimes got in a crowd when you were standing between conversations. On one side of her, James and Will were talking about a rock band Amy had never heard of, and on the other side there was a spirited discussion about politics, which somehow managed to be loud and argumentative despite everyone seeming to agree that everyone in politics was a bastard. Unnoticed by either side, Amy took advantage to slip away from the bar, and headed outside to get some fresh air.

The bracing slap of the cold winter night's air was exactly what she needed. Huddled underneath the Lodge's veranda, she closed her eyes, put her hands on her knees, and took a breath.

Savannah and Morgan... Morgan and Savannah...

Savannah had always been chill with LGBT employees—it was one of the reasons that Amy had jumped at the opportunity to work at Zero Nova to begin with. But despite that, Amy had never seen Savannah actually date anyone. Embarrassingly enough for a lesbian who had never dated in that time herself, she'd assumed that that meant that her boss was straight. Oops.

But if Savannah had that intimate history with Morgan, why had she sent Amy to get the interview instead of doing it herself? Sure, Savannah was the CEO and all, but that didn't mean that she was tied down behind her desk—she was always flitting off to high-profile industry shows and hot celeb events to cover the most choice articles in person.

She could have done it herself. Instead, she'd sent Amy.

"Hey."

Amy shot upwards, her heart pounding hard.

Morgan blinked at her in clear surprise. "Sorry. I didn't mean to startle you." She seemed taken aback in a way that didn't seem to have anything to do with Amy's rabbit-in-the-headlights routine. Her glacier-blue gaze fixed on Amy's face, and she opened her mouth to say something—but then shut it again.

God, how messy was Amy right now, to get that kind of reaction? Amy pressed the backs of her fingers against her cheeks, trying to feel how flushed she was. "Ugh, do I look drunk? I'm not, it's just that the Australians were having a birthday, and it took me way too long to figure out something called Two-Up, which I don't even think is a real thing, by the way..."

"No, no." Morgan cut her off, smiling a little. But something in her eyes seemed hesitant. "It's just that this is the first time I think I've seen you without a full face of makeup."

What? Amy tried to think through the past few days. It was true that she'd shown up to their first interview with professional makeup—of course she had, she knew that that was just how the game went. And then when she'd got ready over the next few mornings, it had involved doing her face in Morgan's bathroom, hadn't it?

She hadn't realized. It was automatic by this stage, even if all that she was going to be doing was writing and playing with dogs.

"It makes you look different."

"Bad different?"

Morgan shook her head. "Definitely not."

What did that mean? Something rose up in Amy's chest like an iceberg of hope. If that line had come out of the mouth of anyone else, Amy would assume that it was flirty...

The Titanic of her common sense rammed into that thought, sending them both sinking into the depths. She's just making polite conversation! God, stop it, you useless lesbian!

She swallowed, then looked away and jerked her thumb over her shoulder. "If you're going in, I'm just warning you that they're probably going to try to make you sing the dirtiest version of the happy birthday song that you know."

Morgan smiled a little. "That's fine. I wasn't going in anyway."

Huh? "You weren't?"

"I just wanted to see if you were here."

Amy's heart felt like it flipped a full 360 degrees in her chest. "Oh?" she said, trying to keep her voice steady. Be chill, Ames. Cool as a cucumber.

"Well, you weren't at home." Morgan shrugged a little. "I wanted to make sure you hadn't got lost on the way here. You'd be surprised how easy it is, with the forest nearby and all."

"Oh." That made sense. Of course it made sense.

Amy had come out to avoid Morgan. Well, that mission was well and truly failed. If she couldn't hide here, then hiding in her room was probably the next best idea. "I was just heading back, anyway," she said.

After a few quick goodbyes to the Aussies, the two of them turned and wandered along the streets. In the half-gloom, snow muffling everything but the sound of their boots, it was like they were in a tiny little universe all of their own.

"How'd the repair job go?"

"Hmm? Oh, it wasn't difficult." Morgan shrugged. "It was just a matter of getting into the ceiling, fixing a couple of holes, and drying everything off. We're going to see if any more leaks spring up overnight, and try to turn the power on tomorrow. Simple as that."

"Simple as that, huh?" Amy rolled her eyes. "I couldn't do something like that, that's for sure. How was Marie?"

A strange look crossed Morgan's face. "Good," she said, cautiously. "We talked for a while. It turns out that we have some interests in common. Why are you smiling?"

Slightly tipsy, Amy couldn't hide the triumphant grin on her face. "What? Nothing. I'm not doing anything."

Her attempt to get Morgan talking to her neighbors had worked! It made a warm little ripple run through Amy.

Over the past few days, Amy had seen another side of Morgan that the townspeople clearly never got to see—and she wasn't even talking about the contents of the sketchbook.

Morgan was funny, and, once you got underneath her icy exterior, she was kind and down-to-earth. But all that everyone else living here got to see of Morgan was her bad case of resting bitch face, and the way that she'd rather keep to herself, leaving social situations as soon as the opportunity arose.

All that Morgan needed was someone to give her a little push, and something in Amy's heart flipped at the thought of being the one to have done that. She'd never thought of herself as someone into being dominant, but something about Morgan made her want to crack a theoretical whip—get out there, hot stuff, and talk to people!

In the moonlight, caught up in her feelings, Amy couldn't stop herself from opening her mouth. "I'm just... I'm just glad that they got to see a different side of you."

"And what side might that be?" Morgan asked, her voice wry.

"The kick-ass, take-charge side. The side that can do anything."

Morgan snorted. "I don't know if I have that side any more."

"I know that you do," Amy said, with feeling.

So much for keeping things normal. She must have sounded strange. Morgan, a few steps ahead, turned to look back at Amy. In the moonlight, her eyes glimmered like something ethereal.

Amy couldn't take her eyes off of her. She stepped forward—

Her boot hit the edge of the curb, hidden under the snow. She stumbled, but before she could trip, Morgan was there, holding her steady.

Amy gazed up at Morgan, pressed up against her. In the new light of the winter moon, she looked like an icy elven queen, something out of this world. Amy's hands tightened on Morgan's.

"Amy..." Morgan said, cautious. "Do you want to kiss me right now?"

Amy's heart raced. "What gives you that idea?"

"The way that you're staring at my mouth," Morgan pointed out, and her voice was even and neutral... but she hadn't yet let go of Amy. There was barely a hand span between them, their breaths turning to fog in the chill of the New Zealand air.

"I could be doing that for a lot of different reasons," Amy said.

Morgan paused, her gaze dropping down to Amy's mouth—just for a fraction of a second, but long enough to make Amy's stomach flip. Then Morgan looked back up to Amy's eyes, with some strange new promise in her voice. "Are you?"

"God, no," Amy said, and then she lurched up, uncaring of how ungraceful the motion was, to press her mouth against Morgan's.

Chapter Fourteen

Amy

Whenever Amy had had sex with someone in the past, it had been with serious, sensible girlfriends. Those relationships had never lasted long—they'd all walked out the door complaining that Amy was too busy for them—but they'd lasted long enough for Amy to get used to how sex went in a relationship. Scheduled date nights. Coming home and sighing in unsexy relief as you took off your shoes and your bras, complaining about the ways that both of them pinched.

This, though... this was different.

They barely made it back inside the cottage before Morgan had Amy up against the wall, her tongue parting her lips. She tasted sugary sweet, like she'd been drinking something raspberry flavored. It was strangely incongruous, out of place with Morgan's demeanor, and the mismatch made Amy laugh a little.

Morgan pulled back just far enough to cock an eyebrow. "Something funny?"

"Nothing," Amy said, and went back for a second taste.

Morgan's hand came up to slide around Amy's neck, her hands falling to Amy's waist, caging her in against the wall. The long lean line of Morgan's body was barely brushing up against Amy, just teasing her.

There was a series of whines, and only one of them was coming from Amy. Amy broke away just enough to turn her head to the side, and found that the two of them were the subjects of a whole packs' worth of attention.

Morgan didn't move her hands from Amy's waist. "Get," she said, in a voice that brooked no doggy disobedience. With resignation, the pack turned away from the interesting game that their master was playing, leaving Amy and Morgan with privacy.

"You're a harsh mistress," Amy laughed breathlessly.

Morgan's mouth brushed against her neck, her chuckle breezing across Amy's bare skin. "That's just the way I am. Do you have any complaints?"

Oh boy. Amy's knees trembled. "Nope. Nuh-uh."

Morgan's hand on Amy's neck stilled, and her voice changed from something promising to something tinged with hesitant concern. "Do you want to take a moment to think about if this is a good idea or not?"

"Oh my god," Amy managed. "Don't you dare."

Morgan sighed in relief. "Good." Her body pressed up against Amy's, collarbone to knee; when Amy moaned, Morgan's thigh pressed in to sink between Amy's legs, parting them for her. Heat rose up through Amy's body, building from her belly up through her chest and to her face, flushed. She sunk her weight down against the hard length of Morgan's thigh. A lightning bolt of arousal shot through her, making her suck in a hard breath.

And then—"Ow!"

Morgan froze, her blue eyes wide. "What's wrong?"

Amy gingerly touched her fingertips to Morgan's snow jacket. "Static shock," she grumbled.

Morgan laughed. Amy had heard her laugh in a lot of different ways over the last few days—sardonic little chuckles, dry little chuffs of amusement, barks of raspy laughter (those ones usually at Amy's misfortune).

This, though, was different. This was open, joyful. Pressed up against each other as they were, when she laughed, the sound reverberated through Amy's body, feeling Morgan's delight as much as hearing it. It made Amy catch her breath.

When Morgan stepped back, breaking their body-to-body connection, Amy let out a whine. "Well, if you want to get shocked again, we can stay like this," Morgan teased. "I didn't know you were into erotic snow-gear play. I didn't know anyone was into that, to be honest."

"Shut up," Amy laughed, and dragged her down the hallway.

The dogs watched them go, tails wagging expectantly at the hopes of treats or pats—but then the humans went into the bedroom and shut the door behind them, and the dogs gave up and settled back down to sleep.

"Get on the bed," Morgan commanded, on the other side of the door, and the tone of her voice and the glint in her eyes sent a shiver running through Amy.

"Ma'am, yes, ma'am!"

"Smartass."

Amy tilted her chin up and batted her lashes. "You like it."

"Hmm." Morgan leaned in, her lips barely brushing against Amy's. "We'll see," she purred, except that Amy knew that that was a lie. Morgan's dark eyes roved from Amy's mouth to her throat, then down to her collarbone, peeking above the hem of her sweater.

Morgan's hands crept up under the hem of Amy's sweater, and Amy shuddered.

"Too much?"

"Too cold."

"Hmm." Morgan's eyes were sharp. "I guess I'll have to warm them up, then."

Morgan Leithe, Amy's brain narrated in reporter mode, is a terrible, cruel woman, who should be banned from seducing innocent journalists.

Relatively innocent journalists, anyway.

Well.... maybe we'll just leave it at 'journalists'.

She bit her lip as Morgan's hands roamed up underneath her sweater, stripping it off of her. Amy flushed pink with a mix of need and embarrassment; if she'd known that she was going to be ravished by a billionaire, she would have worn a nicer bra.

Still, Morgan didn't seem to mind the sight in the slightest. She undid Amy's bra with an engineer's precision, and Amy gasped as the other woman tugged it off, her breasts bared between them.

Amy decided to go on the offensive. She reached up, slipping her hand under Morgan's shirt, ready to pull it off...

...But Morgan pinned Amy's hand down to the bed.

"Hey, c'mon! I want to touch you, too," Amy whined, her back arching up for more of Morgan's hands, her mouth, anything.

"Too bad."

Morgan's cool, amused tone sent a ripple of need running through Amy. She groaned, her hands twisting in the sheets. "But—"

Her appeal was cut off when Morgan dipped her head to take one of Amy's hard nipples into her mouth, teasing it with her tongue slowly, like she had all the time in the world.

"My house, my rules," she said, when she pulled away. "Unless you want to stop?"

"No!" The shout tore its way out of Amy before she could stop herself. "I mean, I, uh."

"Take your time."

Amy let her head fall back against the mattress, and let out a heartfelt groan. "Don't stop," she whispered.

Historically, Amy hadn't been strict on the whole top vs. bottom thing. She'd done everything with her exes and found it all perfectly satisfying— save for wielding a strap, which had turned out to be far beyond the abilities of her shameful core muscles, leaving her doubled-over with a cramp while her then-girlfriend tried not to laugh.

Now, though, with demanding, bossy Morgan calling the shots, she was perfectly content to be a greedy bottom. She stretched herself out along Morgan's bed, and felt a thrill of hot triumph as Morgan's breath visibly quickened at the sight of her. Morgan pinched her nipples a little, making her squeal, and then dropped to her knees between Amy's spread legs.

"Oh, fuck," Amy gasped, as Morgan took her pants off with military precision, and then a few moments later, she was beyond words entirely.

Morgan's tongue laved over her lips, a slow, aching pressure. Her hands stroked lazy stripes along the insides of Amy's spread thighs, holding her open. When Amy shuddered, arching up against Morgan's mouth, Morgan held her still, the firm grip of her hands pinning Amy in place.

Amy didn't know how long it had been since Morgan had been with another woman. Had she had a rebound after Savannah? Did she have a friend with benefits in town? On the face of it, Amy had no way of knowing.

Still, the fiery hunger in Morgan's eyes gave Amy a pretty good idea of how long she'd been pent up. Morgan savored Amy, as in-control as she ever was, but her control was fraying. When Amy bit her lip and arched up for more, Morgan sucked in a shaking breath, the proof of her desire gusting hot against Amy's sensitive skin.

The idea of doing that to someone as cool and collected as Morgan... Amy groaned. She needed more of that, to see the hungry heat that was burning in Morgan's eyes, to feel the possessive desire running through Morgan as she slid her fingers inside of Amy.

Amy rolled her hips up, needing more of Morgan's mouth and those long, sure fingers, and let out a groan as Morgan moved faster, giving Amy everything that she needed.

Then she was coming, wailing helplessly as Morgan's clever mouth and clever fingers worked her through her climax.

Oh my god, she thought, staring at the ceiling and panting. I just banged a billionaire.

If this was how good it felt, no wonder there were all those romance novels about it.

She looked over at Morgan. The older woman was eyeing her cautiously, as if Amy might shriek this was a mistake! and run away.

Nope, no chance of that. In fact...

"I want to touch you," Amy managed, and the slight nod that Morgan gave her was enough to send her fumbling forwards, tugging Morgan down onto the bed. As Morgan let out a laugh, Amy clambered on top of Morgan, still trembling and shaky from her orgasm but eager.

Just because she'd already got hers, didn't mean that she was done.

Morgan was still wearing her pants. How was she still wearing pants?! It took all of Amy's restraint to take enough time to flick Morgan's fly open with a thumb, yanking the zipper apart, and then tugging them off of the other woman's hips in clumsy, hungry desperation.

Morgan let out a low chuckle. A flicker of embarrassment made Amy flush, but she had other things to focus on. As soon as she'd tugged them just barely down enough, baring the slightest stripe of the smooth skin of Morgan's thighs and the flash of unexpected red boyshorts—okay, that was definitely getting filed away for later daydreaming material—she slipped her hand inside Morgan's underwear.

Oh, god, she was wet. Amy hadn't even touched Morgan, but she was wet just from eating Amy out. Amy shuddered, panting hard, and then slid two fingers between Morgan's lips.

The sound of Morgan's sigh was music to Amy's ears. "Keep going," she said, as if anything in the world could make Amy stop at that moment. As she drank in the sensation of Morgan's desire, she leaned down to kiss Morgan, sweet and gentle, then hot and hungry.

Morgan's wetness on her fingers... her clit hard under the pads of her fingers, her slick folds hot... the taste of herself on Morgan's mouth... Morgan's soft moans hitching, stuttering—

And Amy's next climax hit her like a punch, her own cries drowning out Morgan.

Without even being touched.

Um.

Okay.

With her eyes squeezed shut—maybe if you can't see the big scary billionaire, then she can't see you!—Amy didn't know what expression was on Morgan's face, but the low chuckle of laughter and the shift of her body as she looked up at Amy... yeah, she could make a rough guess.

"Amy," Morgan said, a smirk in her voice, "did you just—"

"Quiet!" Amy demanded. "I'm the one that asks the questions, here. Don't come for my job."

And with that, she pressed Morgan back down against the bed.

Chapter Fifteen

Morgan

It had been so long since Morgan had been with another woman.

Before Savannah, she hadn't known what she was missing—not really. She'd known that she was into women, sure, turning her head to track attractive co-workers, thinking about the long legs of a funding backer as she took care of herself later in the night—but all of that had been firmly shut away under lock and key.

She'd been too busy for that, too high-profile to begin to navigate something like a lesbian relationship while in the public eye.

Or so she'd told herself, anyway.

But knowing something intellectually was different to experiencing it in the flesh. It had been easy enough to pretend that that side of herself didn't matter when she'd never had sex with another woman before. After experiencing it for herself, though, feeling the way that someone arched up under your touch, the scent of skin... She couldn't go back to not knowing. That side of her was like a starving wolf, hungry for it.

Over the last few years, she'd known exactly what she'd been missing. She'd locked herself away despite that, and told herself that she wouldn't let it hurt her.

As if that ever worked for a wound.

Amy had broken down her defenses, getting through Morgan's shell with her warmth and her light.

At first, Morgan hadn't wanted it. Now, twined together on her bed, Amy warm and naked and laughing against her mouth, Morgan couldn't think of anything that she wanted more.

Eventually, they managed to get their fill of each other. The warm glow of the moment began to fade, tingeing in with the slight awkwardness of the first time. Amy hesitated, half in and half out of the bed. Morgan could read the question in her body language: should I stay, or should I go?

They didn't know each other—not really. They'd only been together for a handful of days. It would have been completely reasonable for Amy to go back to her own room to sleep. What they'd just done was intimate—to put it lightly—but that kind of thing was different from the intimacy of sleeping together.

Morgan made the decision for the both of them. She looped an arm around Amy and dragged her back down into the bed. Amy squealed a little in surprise, and then laughed.

"You... you want me to sleep here tonight?" she asked, looking up at Morgan. With their new closeness, Morgan could see the details in her dark eyes, the almost amber flecks that peppered her rich brown.

"It's just good hospitality, after all," Morgan said. She tucked Amy up against her, their bodies fitting together.

"Well, you have been a remarkably gracious host..." Amy smirked.

"If you kick me in your sleep, I'm rolling you on to the floor," Morgan said, and pressed a kiss to the back of Amy's neck.

Chapter Sixteen

Amy

Amy awoke to the sound of barking.

Morgan's dogs were ready to go out, she realized. Reason number a hundred why Amy had never wanted dogs.

Mumbling, she rolled over, folding the pillow over her head to cover her ears. Morgan was an early riser; by the time that Amy tended to wake up, Morgan had usually been up for hours. If Amy could stubbornly cling to sleep for just a few more moments, she knew that she'd soon hear the creak of the back door opening, and then the barking would stop, and then Amy could go back to sleep for juuust a few more minutes...

The barking did not stop. Instead, it continued, growing louder... and then Amy let out a squeak as a furry little monster jumped up on her bed, barking happily.

Wait. Scratch that.

It wasn't her bed that Muffin the terrier had jumped up on.

It was Morgan's bed.

And, more importantly, Morgan was in it too.

The awareness of where she was—and exactly how she'd wound up there, and the things that she'd done between those sheets—hit her like a ton of bricks. On autopilot, Amy turned her head with all the grace and elegance of a bad animatronic, and found Morgan smiling up at her from her side of the bed.

Her short blonde hair was fanned out on the pillow, surrounding her face like a halo. Despite being completely naked and still muzzy with sleep, a pillow-crease on her cheek, she still managed to look completely sure of herself. She blinked slowly up at Amy, her blue eyes half-lidded in a smile.

"Oh my god," Amy found herself saying, "you look gorgeous in the morning. Who even looks like that?"

"You, apparently," Morgan tossed back. "Look in a mirror sometime. Good morning to you too, by the way."

Amy flushed. "Oh, shut up." Her hands wrung at the blankets, unsure of whether to draw them up to cover herself, or whether they were past that point.

More precise memories of exactly what she'd done the previous night floated up into her mind. Had she really—and then had Morgan decided to—okay, wow.

Okay, yeah, she was definitely past that point. That point was now so far in the background that she'd need a NASA telescope to locate it. Throwing shame to the wind, Amy dropped the edge of the blanket that she had been clutching.

Morgan made a little tiger-roar sound. It was dizzyingly cute, but Amy still fought the urge to boff her in the face with a pillow.

God, it was sweet. With Morgan's body-warmth still ghosting in her skin, and the beautiful light of a New Zealand morning streaking into the room, Amy shivered. It felt too good, like her body was full of warm honey.

But the moment couldn't last forever. Morgan sighed. "I need to let the dogs out." She swept to her feet in one regal move, completely naked. Despite everything that they'd done, it was the first time that Amy had seen Morgan naked. She swallowed hard, not knowing where to look.

Was it rude to stare at the woman who ate you out so hard you thought you went blind? Was it rude to not stare? Oh my god, her ass—okay, yeah, now Amy was definitely staring.

She shut her open jaw with an audible click. Morgan laughed, and then pulled on her jeans, tossed to the side of the bed. She whistled for the dogs as she slipped on her shoes, and with one inscrutable look back at Amy, headed out.

Left alone in the bed in which she'd just slept with a billionaire, Amy let herself fall backwards, arms outstretched. Yup, this one was just as comfy as the guest bed. She was being spoiled by all these expensive beds—when she got home, her own mattress was going to seem like a torture device in comparison. It served her right for buying a mattress based on podcast recommendations.

And mattress quality wasn't the only way that she'd been spoiled. Amy covered her face with her hands, trying to fight back giggles, and then got to her feet. If she was going to have a morning-after freak-out, she was going to do it in private.

A few minutes later, she was in the shower, availing herself to the fruitiest products that she could find.

Okay, she thought to herself, lathering herself into a cloud of pawpaw-scented bubbles. Take a moment, Ames. Breathe.

I just slept with Morgan freaking Leithe! Ahh!

She fought the urge to giggle, and then lost. Clapping a hand over her mouth to hide the sound, she finally let herself dissolve into first-time morning-after nerves.

Okay, that was not how she'd imagined last night going, but it had been... great! Like, so, so great! And then, instead of waking up and immediately kicking Amy out into the snow, Morgan had seemed just as happy as Amy was!

She slathered herself in guava body wash, her mind spinning. What did that mean? It's not like this was going to be a long-term thing, or, like, a whole deal—the snow had to lift someday, and Amy's bus would come sooner or later, whisking her back to her real life.

But, maybe... maybe this could be something nice, just for now.

That suited Amy just fine. She wasn't after anything serious, and there was no way that Morgan Leithe of all people would be, either.

Still. Amy could definitely stand to volunteer for round two. And maybe three. And, then, depending on how Morgan was feeling, round four onwards...

When she dried her hair, her reflection in the mirror was grinning, her cheeks pink in a way that had nothing to do with the heat of the water. Amy picked up her cosmetics—and then, with a smile, put them back down again.

After she got dressed and stepped out of the bathroom, she only managed to make it a few steps down the hallway before finding Morgan. The older woman stepped out of her private room, almost sharply enough to bump into Amy.

"So, for breakfast—"

Amy's ideas about whipping up pancakes trailed off, half unsaid. Somewhere between Amy getting into the shower and getting out of it again, something had changed in Morgan's expression.

The older woman looked somehow... distant. Wary. Suddenly, Amy felt like she'd been flung from the rosy warmth of this day back to their first meeting, with Morgan's eyes flinty on her across the floor of the Bellbird.

Something twisted in Amy's stomach. She closed her hands into fists. "Um. Is something wrong?"

"Listen," Morgan started. "I just need to make sure that you won't write about this."

Oh. Oh.

Rage ran through Amy, replacing the uncertain nerves. In a way, it was almost welcome: anger was straightforward. "You think I'd put this in the article?"

"I don't know," Morgan said, and Amy hated her a little for how even and steady her voice was. "I don't know much about you at all."

"I'd hoped that you'd know enough to realize that I'm not that kind of person."

"I don't know much about you at all," Morgan repeated. Her voice was gentle, but unmistakably distant. "I just... need to know. I'm a private person."

"You could stand to be a trusting person, too."

Morgan gave Amy an icy stare. Amy tried to hold it, but it was too much. She ground her teeth, and then looked away.

Then all that was between them was silence. There was a moment where Amy thought that Morgan might raise her hand—to touch her arm—but then it passed. Without another word, Morgan stepped away, heading back to let the dogs back in from the yard.

Amy took the opportunity to walk back down the hallway away from her, back into the guest room. She closed the door behind her, then threw herself down on her bed, and pointedly didn't cry. No-one could say she did, not her, nope.

A while later, she opened her eyes again, staring numbly at the ceiling. On the side table, her laptop waited for her.

She had a job to do.

She was a professional. She knew that. All she had to do was to straighten herself up, go out there, and do her job.

Morgan thought that Amy was here for dirt.

Savannah was breathing down Amy's neck.

Amy had to get something juicy, one way or another.

If Morgan thought that Amy was that terrible of a person, why try to prove her wrong? The idea turned Amy's stomach, but something dark in her wounded, aching heart said: if you think I'm that kind of person, why shouldn't I prove you right?

Savannah would like it if she did, that was for sure. A salacious story like that? Zero Nova didn't usually run that kind of angle, but any CEO on the cusp of going broke would slaver for a chance to go with a story like this.

Morgan already expected it to happen, opening her heart just enough for Amy to feel its warmth, and then shutting it again, shoving Amy out in the cold.

Once Amy got this whole mess over and done with, she could take her pick of women back home to sleep with. It was just sex, right? Wasn't she adult enough to handle a one night stand?

But instead of the sex, all that Amy could think of was the wariness in Morgan's eyes as she'd asked Amy to keep it quiet. The way that that wariness didn't quite cover up the fear in the other woman's eyes.

Morgan thought Amy was going to hurt her.

Amy knew that she should.

She sat on the guest room bed for a long time, just staring out of the window. Outside, the snow continued to fall—but lighter, now, than the day before. The sky was bluer, the sun reflecting off of the sheer white of the snow, making the scene feel almost cheery and bright.

Her fingers tapped their way across her keyboard. The snow's not letting up, Savannah. There are some logistical issues. I need more time to deal with this. Could we push the deadline back a little?

Amy had to give it to Savannah: it never took long to get an answer from her, even if it was one that you didn't want.

People who can't do their jobs don't get promotions.

No second chances.

Chapter Seventeen

Amy

"Three... two... one!"

Morgan, her toolbox open on a cafe table in front of her and grease stains smudged along her forearms, flicked the light switch. The gathered locals let out a cheer as the Bellbird lights turned back on—and stayed on. Amy leaned against the wall and clapped along with the rest of them.

"You're a lifesaver!" Kaia said with joy. Before Morgan could reply, Kaia grabbed her by the arms and pressed a kiss to her cheek.

Morgan Leithe, mysterious and powerful billionaire, spluttered awkwardly. Amy couldn't help but laugh, and then laughed harder as Morgan shot her an icy glare.

As the crowd began to chat, congratulating Marie, Morgan peeled away from them to join Amy, nodding politely at the praise that was aimed her way.

"Phew. I'm sure glad that worked," Amy said, when they were together again. "I wouldn't have wanted to try to eat that much bacon." She eyed the busy crowd. "But good thing that it went off without a hitch, huh? That's a lot of pressure."

Morgan smiled a satisfied little smile to herself. "Old pro trick: always test something quietly before the big reveal. I made sure it was working earlier this morning."

"You cheater."

Morgan raised her hands in placation. "Hey, it worked, didn't it?"

Amy let out a snort of laughter. The mood between them was strained, but it was hard not to get swept up by the cheer of the locals.

Amy took a breath and forced herself to smile. She elbowed Morgan gently. "I hope you skipped breakfast, because by the look of things we're going to have to have some celebratory hotcakes, and Marie doesn't skimp on the jam—"

"Hey, good good people, have you heard the good good news?" Will held his phone over his head. "The roads are gonna reopen tomorrow!"

The news hit Amy like a slap in the face.

That was... faster than she'd expected.

Except that it wasn't, actually. She'd been trapped in town for days. Of course the roads were going to open soon.

Maybe it was just faster than she'd hoped.

Amy looked over to Morgan, needing to see the other woman's reaction —but the expression on the older woman's face was unreadable, cool and distant.

As the locals all began to chat about what they needed to do in the larger surrounding towns, all kinds of odd jobs and to-do lists backing up, Morgan stepped a little closer to Amy. To a casual observer, it was nothing of note, but the angle of their bodies as they faced each other formed a closed-off little bubble separate to the joy of the rest of the room.

"Would you like to go for a walk?" Morgan asked, her voice perfectly casual. "There's a river nearby that's beautiful this time of year."

Amy tried to smile. "Sounds nice. Lead the way."

They walked in silence, which suited Amy just fine for once. The river turned out to be just over the road, a few minutes' walk away.

Amy had woken up that morning to find a sky that was nearly entirely blue, peppered with a few small clouds that skittered quickly across the sky as if embarrassed to be ruining the view.

The first half of Amy's stay in the town had been harried by Morgan's disappearing act, and the second half had mostly involved huddling indoors. Despite the amount of time she'd spent in Ohakune, she hadn't actually done a lot of sightseeing.

The river ran down from the mountain, then through the woods that surrounded the town. The trees were thick, mossy pines, but underneath them was a thick wall of plants that looked almost tropical—but that were covered in snow.

"Woah," Amy said, looking at the snowy ferns that boxed her in. "You know, I'm not exactly a hiking-boots-and-granola-bars type, but I'd kind of just assumed that woods were woods no matter where you went. But this? This looks prehistoric."

Morgan let out a chuckle. "Welcome to New Zealand."

They soon reached a bridge and settled against its railing, watching the crystal-clear water of the river run by beneath them. When Morgan spoke up again, it was about the one thing more complicated than the tangled mess of emotions that was running between the two of them. "How's your article going?"

"God." Amy made a vague noise, wobbling her hand back and forth in the universal gesture of who even knows? "I have... something. That's mostly done. This hasn't exactly been the easiest assignment," she laughed, a tinge of bitterness in her voice.

"Because—"

"Not because of that, thank you very much." Amy tossed her hair. "I don't make a habit of sleeping with my interviewees."

Morgan's mouth curled up in a wry smile. "Their loss."

Amy let out a snort of laughter despite herself. "Flatterer."

It would have been easy enough to keep the conversation light and flirty, pretending that yesterday hadn't happened. Still, there was a topic that Amy had to circle around and bring up, no matter how much she wanted to leave it buried.

Did she need to know for the interview? For herself?

She didn't know any more.

"But you're wrong," she continued. "Going by the evidence, anyway. Ask any of my exes how long it took before they walked out the door. You won't hear any large numbers there. I'm not exactly a catch."

If Morgan had been any of Amy's friends or colleagues, Amy was sure she would have given her a brush-off line like You'll find the right woman one day! or The time just wasn't right, Ames!

Instead, she just cocked her head, inviting Amy to continue. "Oh?"

"Everyone I've dated liked the whole boss bitch thing, and they liked telling their friends that I was a cool, hip reporter, but then we got closer and... I guess they realized that that was all there was to me." She looked down at the river. "My life isn't made for two."

"You settled into life here easily enough," Morgan said, then chuckled. "Even with the dogs, and that's no small ask. You managed life in this town easier than I did, that's for sure."

"It took a snowstorm to keep me from working to my schedule!" Amy laughed. "And now, vroom, I'm outta here. Back to the grind. No space for someone else in my life."

"Maybe instead of that... someone else's life could have space for you."

Amy's heart raced. "Pfft, I'll believe that when I see it," she managed.

Morgan sighed a world-weary sigh. "Love can be hard," she said, simply.

Here was her chance. Amy tightened her fingers on the railing of the bridge, and took it. "Even for you?"

"Even for me." Morgan laced her fingers together, looking down into the river.

Amy felt what Morgan was going to say before she even opened her mouth. The way she hunched her shoulders, the line between her eyebrows...

Somewhere along the line, the things that Amy could read in Morgan's body language had changed. Instead of cold, she saw hesitant; instead of cruel queen of ice hell she saw unsure. Wary. Hurt.

"I was in a relationship, once."

Morgan looked up from her laced fingers, looking Amy in the eyes. "And I do mean once. I kept that door firmly shut. I knew what was behind it, but I thought that it... didn't fit my life. I thought I could just keep that part of me shut away forever."

"That doesn't work."

"No, it sure didn't." Morgan looked back to her hands, and the river beneath them. "Sooner or later someone got through my defenses." She smiled a wry little smile, the sort that had no humor in it whatsoever.

Amy's heart was hammering. "Oh?"

"And then," Morgan continued, as breezy as if she was talking about the weather, "she blackmailed me."

"What?!"

Amy had been trying her hardest to sneak up on the topic, to get Morgan to talk about her relationship with Savannah without tipping her off—without letting Morgan know that Amy had been snooping.

This, though, was not something she'd been prepared for.

Morgan didn't seem to notice anything strange about Amy's reaction. "Mm-hmm."

"Was that why you disappeared?"

"Got it in one."

"But..." Amy's hand rose automatically to touch Morgan on the shoulder.

Amy had left her family behind when she'd got the hell out of her hometown, and nothing of value had been lost. Without anyone to hide anything from any more, she'd been as openly gay as she'd wanted to. Sure, she'd got some flack here and there—some new acquaintances had tried the 'oh, don't be close-minded', or 'that's really trendy now, isn't it?', or even the classic that was 'maybe you just haven't met the right man yet...'; a promising job interview had been followed by an unexpected rejection email, hinting that a certain something on her social media had been an issue.

She wasn't an idiot. She knew that the higher the ladder you climbed, and the closer you got to the old boy's club, the more kickback you'd get. Still...

"But... if she spilled her guts, that still wouldn't have been enough to stop you from doing business, right? Way worse scandals than that come out all the time. Even faster these days, with everyone putting each other on blast on Twitter. Sure, it'd suck, but everyone would move on from gossiping about it in, like, a week. Two, max."

"It wasn't about the business." Morgan didn't hesitate. "Or the gossip. It was about... love."

Well, yeah? "Yes...? That's what she was blackmailing you about, right?"

"Not just that. Not just love for her. Love for... everything." Morgan laced her fingers together and gazed off at the mountains in the distance. "I realized that I didn't love her any more—and I didn't love anything else, either. Inventing used to thrill me... but when I took stock in that moment, I realized that somewhere along the line, I'd grown tired of it. Everything in my life was just the way it was because of obligation."

She shrugged one lean shoulder. "So I stepped away from it all."

"Wow, I've seen some pretty gnarly breakups, but you broke up with the entire world all at once."

Morgan gave her a wry smile and rapped her knuckles on the bridge. "Not this part of it."

"I guess not." Amy gazed down into the water. "Wow. I never knew..."

Morgan gave her a shrewd look. "You know, I wasn't sure of that, at first. I thought you were here because of it. Because of her."

Is she testing me?

Don't trip up, Ames.

Her heart hammering, Amy screwed her eyebrows up. "Huh? How would I know her?"

Morgan held her gaze for a moment, and then dropped it back to the river. "You're a journalist. I thought maybe you'd figured something out about it. Maybe that's why you chased me down."

That's a lie, Amy thought, dizzy. All of Morgan's cool disdain and wariness when they'd first met...

...she'd thought that Amy was a plant. Savannah had blackmailed Morgan, and then sent Amy straight to her door. It was reasonable for Morgan to think that Amy was someone that Savannah had sent to try to... mess with her? To keep tabs on her?

Amy's guts churned.

"Wow." Amy said, not looking Morgan in the eyes. "And I thought I took breakups badly."

Morgan laughed, and then pushed herself away from the bridge. "Come on," she said. "Let's go back. It's getting cold."

ele

Later, back home—no. Amy caught herself. Back at Morgan's home, she checked the time zone app on her phone, and then shut the guest room door.

Taking a deep breath, she made a call.

"Savannah," she said, a moment later. "I know that you two used to be involved."

Chapter Eighteen

Amy

There was a moment of silence, and Amy waited, bracing herself for instantly being fired. Instead, though, Savannah made a low, amused sound.

"Hmm. She actually said so?"

"Not in so many words."

Savannah laughed. "Oh, you are a good little investigator, after all. Well done."

Amy clenched her teeth. "I need to know why you sent me here."

"No, you don't." From the other side of the world, Savannah's voice was as breezy as if she was chatting about margin width, or what cuisine to order for an office lunch. "I gave you your assignment, and unless blizzards can cause amnesia, you should still remember the details."

"Savannah," Amy hissed. "I can't do a good job if you send me in blind."

"Oh, fine." Savannah sighed dramatically. "If you've got this much of a hunger for honesty, remind me never to let you loose near my taxes or the contents of my shapewear drawer."

It was an opening. Amy's palms were clammy. "You two... dated?" It wasn't exactly the term that those racy illustrations had suggested, but it was the safest word for her to spring for. "And then you blackmailed her?"

"This isn't Jeopardy. Answers do not come in the form of a question."

Amy felt a sudden wave of gratitude for the distance that was separating them; if they were in the same room, she was certain she would have throttled her boss. "Savannah Whitney, 26. You had a secret relationship with Morgan Leithe, ending when you blackmailed her for enough money for you to start your own magazine."

"Correct! And if you share this tidbit around, I will sue the skin right off of you and wear it as a coat."

"I like my skin where it is just fine, thanks." That was no idle threat. Amy did not relish the idea of having cut-throat little Savannah as an enemy. "I just need to know where this interview plays into that history, Savannah. A slap in the face to an ex? Getting your foot in the door for some reconciliation? Work with me, here."

Savannah let out a harsh bark of laughter at the mention of reconciliation. "Oh, Amy, you've met Morgan—do you think she's the kind of person who would want to get back together after all this?"

"I think she'd sooner burn your house down," Amy said, honestly.

"No, she'd rather burn her own house down, and then go live in the woods like a hobo." Savannah sounded... exasperated, Amy realized.

"You didn't predict that she'd quit," she ventured.

"Who would?! I just thought she'd give me the money and then break up with me, and we would go on to be fabulously cold to each other at parties. But no, she had to act the martyr and run away, and now if I need anything else from her, I apparently need to chase her half-way around the world."

If Savannah needed anything else... Amy thought back to the empty desks in Zero Nova. "You're running out of money."

"We're running out of money," Savannah corrected. "What would you do, if you ran your own company? Would you let it go under, or would you track down your ex and strong-arm her into giving you a real cash-cow of an interview? Just one little interview. Would you do that to stay in the game?"

Amy was silent.

"That's what I th—"

"Did you ever love her?"

It was a pathetic little question, and it slipped out of Amy before she realized it. It seemed to take Savannah aback, because it left silence in its wake.

"Yes," she said, simply, after a while. Amy had never heard Savannah's voice like that before: stripped down of jaunty bitchiness and effervescent snobbiness, she just sounded... normal. A woman who was tired, her voice strained around the edges. "I did, I think. Who wouldn't?"

"But," she continued, "I did what I had to do. What was our future going to be? She was never going to come out, let alone acknowledge that we were an item. Wrinkly old men will step out with younger women, but Morgan? Never."

"But... blackmail?"

Amy could almost hear the way that Savannah shrugged casually. "We fought, and I was so, so angry... the threat just kind of slipped out of me. Then she took me up on it! I wasn't actually expecting it. And that was that." There was a pause, then a laugh. "You must have felt something like that, spending that much time with her. She shuts down out of nowhere. The woman's infuriating."

Shame twisted in Amy's chest. To begin with, she had been frustrated with the way that Morgan was running hot and cold on her, just like Savannah had guessed.

But who could blame Morgan for pulling away and being cautious when she was surrounded by people like Savannah?

"Getting cranky about your relationship problems is one thing," Amy said. "Committing a federal crime is another."

"Potatoes, tomatoes—or however that saying goes." Savannah gave a low, thoughtful hum. "It's strange... You know what I heard as soon as you started talking? Emotion."

Amy felt her blood run cold. She did not like the tone in Savannah's voice. "Yes?" she blithered, with a detachedness she didn't feel. "Of course I'm getting emotional. Who wouldn't be cranky after being snowed in in the most boring town on the planet? If you ever want to diversify and get into tourism writing, I already have an article waiting for you on the Top Ten Most Boring Monuments To Vegetables."

Savannah ignored her. "I haven't heard you sound this upset since the time Georgia sniped your contact on that iPhone article. Amy, Amy," Savannah said, thrilled. "Are you nursing a little bit of a crush?"

"What? Pfft." Amy was glad that she hadn't made this a video call. "I've only been here a few days, what kind of girl do you take me for?"

"One that's exactly her type."

And she was, wasn't she? She'd carefully modeled herself after Savannah, trying to be the best little reporter that she could be.

A chill ran through Amy. "Wait, is that why you sent me here?"

"Would you believe me if I said it wasn't?"

"Nope."

"Then let's skip that and move on. I could have sent Georgie in your place, sure. But the more incredible an interview is, the better... and you're exactly Morgan's type. I know, because you're so much like me."

Amy could almost hear the way that Savannah was smirking over the phone. "And now here you are, angry that I sent one of my best writers to write my best story, defensive over the honor of some crabby billionaire... Well. It makes a girl wonder what exactly has been going on over there, is all."

"You sent me over here to seduce her?"

"Of course not! I hire professional snoops, not sex workers. That'd just be asking to get the pants sued off of me." There was a small pause as Savannah clearly rolled her eyes. "But, you know, if something were to happen, all on its own, then, well..."

Amy's palms were damp with sweat. If Savannah asked if she and Morgan had already slept together, Amy wasn't sure that she'd be able to lie convincingly.

Thankfully, Savannah didn't seem to notice. "Well, then you'd have journalism gold on your hands, wouldn't you?" she continued. "More people will pick up a tech mag for gossip on celebrity figures than for specs or actual longform reporting, these days. Just a hopeful little idea."

Amy felt sick.

She was sitting in Morgan's house, which Morgan had opened up to Amy despite everything, and here she was, a tool of the person who'd broken her heart.

No wonder Morgan was wary. No wonder she was hurt.

Amy deserved every ounce of distrust Morgan had shown her.

"Stop navel-gazing," Savannah said. "I can hear it."

"I'm just looking at my notes," Amy lied.

"Mm-hmm." Savannah's tone made no bones about letting Amy know that she saw right through her. "Listen, this is business. You want to make it in the industry, you use whatever—and whoever—you can. You haven't had a problem with that up to this point, have you?"

Amy stayed silent.

"Let me make it easy for you," Savannah continued, as easy as if she'd had this conversation with other fledgling reporters many times. For all that Amy knew, maybe she had. "You can choose to give up on this assignment, if your conscience is really troubling you that much."

"But?"

"See, you do have instincts. But you can kiss your job here goodbye."

It was what Amy had expected. She shut her eyes—but Savannah wasn't done.

"And without your job—and, of course, without a reference from me, don't pretend that you thought for a moment that I'd be generous—you won't be able to keep that apartment. I know you don't have parents with deep pockets like some of the other kids here to bankroll your rent. And without a job, an apartment... what will you have? Do you really want to roll the dice on being able to start over from scratch again, now that you've made it so far? In this economy?"

Amy didn't say anything. Couldn't say anything.

"Look, Amy, I'm not saying anything that you don't already know. Come on. Be realistic. There's a reason I hired you, and I'd hate to see those talents go to waste in assfuck nowhere. Think of this like a hurdle that everyone in the industry has to jump over."

Savannah's voice was resolute. "You worked hard to get where you are. Take what's yours. C'mon, rub it in Georgie's face."

Amy held the phone to her ear and stared out of the window. Ahead of her, the town stretched out, sleepy and quiet in its coat of white.

It was like something out of a fairy-tale.

But her role in this story had always been to be the monster.

Chapter Nineteen

Morgan

Morgan had lived the last three years of her life independent and unburdened by timetables. With the exception of letting the dogs in and out, she was used to doing whatever she felt like at any time—reading, trying her hand at a new craft, or simply relaxing, soaking in her little woodshed tub with a nice bottle of wine and drinking in the sight of some of the best scenery on the planet.

It had been a long time since she'd had to pay attention to the clock.

On that day, though, the sight of the time ticking down seemed inescapable.

5.30 am, her bedside alarm clock said, when the dogs began to whuffle at her to be let out.

6.00 am, the angle of the sun said, beaming through the bathroom window when she got out of her morning shower.

7.00am, the little readout on the microwave said, when Amy wandered into the kitchen. She wasn't wearing makeup, this time, and Morgan could read the smudges under her eyes like a book. She hadn't got much sleep, either.

"Good morning," Morgan said.

"Morning," Amy replied in kind. Her eyes cut to the microwave clock, but she didn't say anything about it.

"Have you got much planned for today?"

Amy's mouth quirked to the side. "Not exactly."

"You should try to see a little more of the town," Morgan said. "It's a shame to come all the way out here and then spend all of your time without seeing it."

"Heh, true."

A silence stretched out between the two of them. When it was done, Amy took her coffee and turned to leave. "I guess I'll—"

"I'm sorry about what I implied, before. What I said."

The memory of what she'd said, of Amy's reaction, made Morgan feel sick—what kind of monster had she become, that her first thought about being shown some affection was that the other person was only doing it for some agenda?

"I don't think that you're going to write about it," she said, reaching out to take Amy's hands in hers. "I'm just... not good at trusting people, these days."

Amy flinched, and then let out a strange, bitter laugh. "There's nothing wrong with being cautious."

"There's such a thing as being too cautious," Morgan started, but the rest of what she was about to say was cut off Amy stepped forward and covered her mouth with her own.

This early in the morning, she still tasted a little like toothpaste, but it was one of the sweetest kisses that Morgan had ever had. Amy kissed her with a deep longing, her eyes fluttering shut with a sigh.

Then, just as Morgan was about to draw her in for more, Amy pulled back, her eyes downcast. "Sorry! Sorry. I just got a little greedy."

"You don't have anything to be sorry for."

"God, stop being so perfect!" Amy rolled her eyes. She stepped away. "This is a bad idea. I'm leaving in a few hours."

"I know. I'm not asking you to stay. Just because I stepped away from everything, that doesn't mean that I think everyone else wants to, too." Morgan closed the gap between the two of them, taking Amy into her arms.

Amy hesitated, caught on the precipice of some internal war... but then leaned into her with a sigh.

"But maybe..." Morgan continued, "maybe you can take some nice memories with you, when you go."

Amy laughed. This time, it sounded normal again. "Usually when people make nice memories on holiday, it's snow and scenery, not..."

"Not...?"

"Well, I don't know." Amy looked up and gave her a tired, cheeky grin. This close, Morgan could count every freckle on her face. "Whatever you've got on your mind right now."

The first time, they'd been driven by haste, wanting each other too much to slow down, throwing themselves at each other so that neither of them would have the time to say 'this is crazy, we should stop'.

Now, though, even though the seconds were slipping away, they took their time. Morgan pressed Amy against the countertop, kissing her deeply.

When Amy had kissed her just a few moments ago, she'd seemed conflicted. There was something strained in her eyes, some internal war going on beyond Morgan's reach.

But now, in Morgan's arms, she seemed to have put her worries to the side for a moment. Amy melted into her arms, fitting against Morgan like she was made for her, and kissed her back. Her hands wrapped around Morgan's waist, and she leaned into her with a sigh.

Standing there together in Morgan's little, warm cottage kitchen, it was like they were never meant to be anywhere else. It was like Amy was fated to blow into town, to force her way into Morgan's walled-off little life and to pry her out of her shell; it was like Amy was fated to kiss her, sweet and warm, in the middle of her kitchen, tasting vaguely of toothpaste.

Morgan gripped her tighter, pulled Amy closer against herself. She closed her eyes, cutting off the sight of the microwave clock.

Amy was about to leave. They were nothing to each other, really—they'd only known each other for a few days.

But even if this wasn't supposed to last, Morgan still wanted to savor it.

Morgan slid her hands up inside Amy's t-shirt, feeling a thrill of satisfaction run through her as Amy shivered from her touch.

"You know," Amy grumbled, "I usually dress much better than this. High label, tailored, the works. You're missing out on the full Amy Kelly experience." She glared down at the tourist t-shirt she was wearing. "God! I'm going to have to do some Inception shit to remove this particular detail from my memories, I think."

Morgan laughed, and then nipped at her ear. "You don't want to remember having sex in a shirt with a dancing cartoon rutabaga on the front?"

"No, I don't!" Amy tried to keep her furious face, but dissolved into giggles. "What if it awakens something in me? What if I start getting horny the next time I walk down the produce aisle? I don't need that."

"Let me help you out, then," Morgan said. As Amy laughed, she whisked the offending item of clothing off of Amy's body, throwing it over her shoulder to land somewhere on the floor.

"Any other problems?"

"Hmm..." Amy settled her hands on Morgan's hips, looking up at her through her lashes with a devilish smile. "Maybe a change of location?"

ele

The dogs were left cocking their heads in confusion as Amy and Morgan went outside, shutting the door firmly behind them. No snow booties? No playtime? No new friend to throw tennis balls for them?

Eventually, they gave up, accepting that they had been cruelly abandoned, and fell asleep in one giant furry pile on the rug.

ele

The outside bath was at its best in the evening, a glass of wine in hand, the mountain range on the horizon, and the stars shining overhead, blindingly bright this far away from the big city.

Still, mornings had their own charm, too.

A fine fog wreathed Mount Ruapehu in an ethereal halo, frost crisping the air. It was the work of a moment for Morgan to fill the tub and set the fire underneath it, as Amy perched on the side of the heavy iron tub, swinging her feet with a soft smile on her face. She trailed her fingers in the water, testing.

When it was warm enough, she stood and stripped off her clothes.

Morgan hadn't really got to see much of Amy's body. Sure, she'd got her naked—but her mind had been on other things, and then they'd snuggled down and fallen asleep... and then Morgan had ruined everything by letting her suspicious nature take charge.

Now, though, in the early morning light, she finally had a chance to take in every inch of her.

"Like what you see?" Amy teased. She looked down at herself, and gave a little shimmy. "This is all thanks to a lot of time at the gym, the personal trainer from hell, and a meal plan rigid enough to scare an astronaut." She paused, then poked a roll, pouting. "Well, not that bit. That bit's thanks to all those big meals and spiced mead at the Lodge, and sitting around your cottage all day."

"I like that bit just as much," Morgan said, her voice full of feeling.

Amy stared up at her, and then looked away, snorting. She stepped in to the tub and—

"Cold!" she yelped, jumping back.

Morgan laughed. She slid her shirt off, noting the way that Amy's eyes tracked every move, and then followed it with her pants, setting them to the side.

She liked to think that she had always been practical about her body. It was a thing that carried her brain around from meeting to meeting, occasionally demanding fuel and maintenance. She'd gotten into the habit of taking care of it not for vanity's sake, but for sheer efficiency: the healthier she was, the fewer days she'd have to spend off sick, waiting to get back to her workshop to pick her projects back up.

Still, it was hard not to feel a little inadequate next to Amy's gym bunny body. A little skinny, maybe, on the bony side of things.

"You're gorgeous," Amy said, her eyes sparkling. She stepped back into the water with a shiver. "Brr."

Morgan slid into the tub. "Oh, it'll get warmer."

Amy shifted aside and made room for her. When setting the outdoor bath up, Morgan had gone out of her way to track down a tub that was big enough to stretch out in. She had experienced enough sardine-can baths in her life to never want to deal with cold knees or cramped elbows ever again.

Little did she know at the time that she'd also be choosing something that was big enough to fit two people at once. There were unexpected benefits of dreaming big.

Amy smirked up at Morgan as she settled in next to her. Her hair was already damp in places, clinging to her cheeks and neck. "Smooth, real smooth."

"Well, I was talking about the fire, but if you insist..."

Morgan kissed her, slow and warm.

Amy was leaving. But maybe that didn't mean that Morgan should shut herself away from her negative feelings, drawing away.

Maybe it meant that she should lean into it, instead, and enjoy every moment without regret.

"What are you smiling at?" Amy blinked.

"Nothing. Just you."

Amy blew a raspberry. "That's cheesy. Try harder."

"Hmm." Morgan looked down the length of Amy's body, wearing nothing but the shimmer of the water's surface and the reflection of the sky. "How about..."

In one swift move, Morgan reached out and hooked an arm around Amy's waist. Amy let out a squeal as she was tugged up on top of Morgan.

"Cold!" Amy shivered, now exposed to the winter air. She snuggled up closer to Morgan as Morgan lay back against the tub, the two of them sinking under the surface of the water.

Morgan gazed up at her. "I'm smiling at someone who throws tennis balls for rescue dogs and plays superhero to small local businesses."

Amy dropped her eyes, but let out a snort of laughter seemingly despite herself. "That was all you," she corrected her.

"Nope." Morgan shook her head, her hands settling on Amy's waist above her. "If it was just me, I wouldn't have even known they needed help, let alone felt like I should go help them out." She chuckled. "And now I'm part of a book club. I think."

"And you got some bacon out of the deal, too. Books and bacon—what else do you need in life?"

The heated look in Morgan's eyes took a turn for the wicked. "Well, I can certainly think of a few things...."

Morgan slid a thigh between Amy's legs, and Amy parted her knees in eager response. "Oh?" she teased. "Well, I'm all ears."

Amy ground down against Morgan's thigh, and Morgan felt the shudder that ran through her. Instinctively, she arched up against Amy herself, pressing the two of them inseparably close, their bodies grinding together in a sweetly aching push and pull. When Amy rocked her hips down, Morgan rolled up to meet her, both moving in one slow, building wave.

Morgan slid her hand down over the curve of Amy's ass, tracing the path of her body around and down. Her fingers slipped between Amy's slick folds, caressing her as she ground down against Morgan's thigh. Amy let out a throaty gasp, her hands trembling on Morgan's shoulders.

In response to the sound of her own gasp, Amy bit her lip.

"You don't need to stay quiet," Morgan reassured her.

"I'm going to trust you that there are no peeping toms around," Amy said, "but no, nuh-uh, no way am I screaming your name outside. What if, I don't know, a neighbor is passing by? What if a lost hiker is stumbling to your door for help, finally glad to be back safely in civilization? Do you think they want to hear me moaning fuck me harder, Morgan Leithe?" She cocked her chin towards the mountain. "What if I set off an avalanche? People could get hurt because you were too good with your fingers."

Morgan laughed, her shoulders shaking. "You're ridiculous."

"I know." Amy beamed.

When Amy had first sat down in her cottage and tried to interview her, Morgan had recognized the smile on her face instantly. It was all Savannah, a carefully workshopped press-conference smile that gave no trace of the thoughts underneath it.

You could tell something about a person by their smile. Morgan had wanted to see Amy's real smile. She'd traded three truths for it, days ago.

It was worth trying to see. When she was happy—really, truly happy— Amy's real smile was a little crooked, a little goofy; it was the sort of thing that you'd hate to see in a candid photo of yourself, the sort of thing that people would make a fuss over, saying oh my god, do I smile like that all the time?

But it was all Amy, bright and a little over the top.

It was perfect.

"What are you looking at?" Amy teased, a little flustered by the attention. Between the warmth of the fire, the embarrassment of being gazed adoringly at, and the movement of Morgan's fingers, she was going pink from her head to her toes, her ears flushed deliciously warm.

Amy ran her hands up along Morgan's sides, stroking her from hip to waist to ribs, and then she planted her hands on Morgan's breasts. Her eyes fell half-lidded in satisfaction as she took her fill, her hands moving in a rolling back-and-forth, gently caressing them.

The warm water and the cold air agreed with Amy. Her skin flushed and her ears pink, her eyes dark with a hungry need, she looked thoroughly ravishable. Morgan stroked Amy's offered sex as she ground down against her hand, Morgan's fingers running greedily along her, dipping just inside the slick kiss of her lips to tease her clit and drag across her hole, then backing out again to run through her curls.

There were so many things that Morgan wanted to do to Amy, but there was no time for toys or ropes, let alone bringing her close to the verge and then keeping her there until she couldn't bear it any more. She sucked hungry, hot kisses along the wet curve of Amy's neck, one hand on her hip dragging her down against the length of Morgan's thigh, the other slipping two fingers inside her.

Amy's hands slipped and scudded over Morgan's body as she gasped, too close to her climax for control, desperate to cling to Morgan for more. She threw herself down on top of Morgan, their breasts pressing together, and tried to slip a hand down between Morgan's legs to reciprocate.

Morgan arched her back to give her the space she needed, and Amy's fingers eagerly slid between her lips, making her moan.

It was the snowball that caused the impending avalanche. "Oh, fuck!" Amy's legs clamped down on Morgan's at the sound of her moan, her thighs trembling. She threw her head back, the wet curls of her hair clinging to her shoulders, and came with a cry.

Morgan held her through the aftershocks, luxuriating in the way that Amy's body clenched around her fingers, searingly hot. Then Amy was done; she flopped bonelessly back under the water, groaning.

Morgan wasn't someone who needed perfect reciprocation. Making pretty women come was its own reward. Staying in control, making them lose theirs—it was the way she liked it.

But Amy wasn't entirely done, and as she cupped the soft mound of Morgan's sex in her hand, Morgan couldn't bring herself to mind.

"Mmm," Amy hummed, her eyes half-lidded and heavy with bliss. She slid her fingers into Morgan's wet heat, her thumb on the stiff, aching peak of her clit. Her movements were languid, satisfied, but there was still an eager heat behind them.

Amy kept her eyes on Morgan's face as she touched her, no teasing, no fumbling, just a steady, building simplicity, their bodies tangled together.

"You're quiet," Morgan said, fighting the growing need to pant for breath.

"I'm just enjoying the show," Amy said with a cheeky grin up at her.

Morgan took Amy's chin in her hands and tilted it up. Amy let out a peal of laughter, but it was cut off as Morgan kissed her, hot and demanding.

Amy's fingers moved faster, her body writhing against Morgan's. It was everything Morgan needed, everything she wanted. Morgan came with a growl against Amy's sweet kiss, Amy stroking her through it until she was left boneless, Amy pressed to her chest.

They lay there for a while, enjoying the warmth of the water contrasting against the chill of the winter air, tangled together. Pressed up against her, Morgan could feel Amy's heart beating in her chest, slow and steady.

How long had it been since she'd had a moment like this? Sure, she knew how long it had been since she'd last slept with a woman—but even with Savannah, had Morgan ever had a moment like this one?

She closed her eyes, tilting her head back towards the sky. She wasn't sure.

Her head knew that this was nothing more than a fling.

Her heart disagreed.

"Well, those were some pretty good memories to take away, as memories go," Amy snickered, after a while. "They don't put that on the brochures."

Morgan looked over at Amy, her head pillowed on her arm, her hair falling around her face. The early morning sunlight that was slanting through the clouds caressed her features in stripes, dappling her, making her dark eyes glimmer with a rich warmth.

"Hmm." Morgan sat up, eyeing Amy. "Humor me for a moment, will you?"

"Huh? Sure." Amy blinked.

It was the work of a moment for Morgan to get up, as wet and naked as the day she was born, and to disappear into the house, ignoring the goosebumps that raced over her body. She swept through the door of her art room to rifle through the assorted detritus to grab—ah, there.

In a minute, she was back in the yard, a sketchpad and pencil in hand. "There are other ways of making memories, too," she said, with a smile.

Chapter Twenty

Amy

"Come here," Morgan had said. "Let me draw you."

And, really, how could Amy have turned her down?

After a brief moment to towel themselves off and throw some clothes back on, she brushed snow off of the stump in the backyard and settled herself on it.

In any other time in her life, a camera pointed at her was like a magic spell: it made her suck in her gut, smile the practiced smile that she knew looked best, and angle her face upwards just so. Now, though, she didn't feel any of those urges. What was the point? Morgan had seen her without any of that posturing, and she'd liked what she'd seen regardless. Amy simply sat and let herself relax.

Amy turned her face upwards, letting her eyelashes fall shut. Fat soft snowflakes settled on her skin with tiny pinpricks stings of cold, melting against her face.

Underneath the warm wool of the handmade shawl she'd borrowed, she twisted her fingers together. "It's still snowing a little. Are you sure that the bus will run in this?"

"Mm." For a moment, Amy thought that Morgan hesitated—but maybe that was just a regular lull in between strokes. The other woman's arm kept moving, and she didn't look up. "They finished plowing the connecting road between here and the main road. There's still a lot of snow on the ground in town, and a fair bit more is going to fall tonight, but that's a problem for here. The road that'll take you out of town is clear."

Amy tilted her head up to the sky and sighed. "I wouldn't mind if it snowed again."

"I bet your boss might have opinions about you spending another week in a ski town instead of behind a desk."

"My boss has a lot of opinions about everything," Amy said. "I don't want to think about them right now."

"Mmm." The corners of Morgan's eyes crinkled with laughter, though her drawing hand never stopped moving. "Maybe we could do a rain dance."

"I find that getting my hair done and stepping outside usually makes it rain," Amy agreed. "We could try that."

"We could do a load of laundry."

"Plan a picnic," Amy agreed.

"Wash the car."

"You could tie me up."

"Oh? And what makes you think I'd be into that kind of thing?"

Laughing, Amy looked up at Morgan through her lashes. "Oh, don't pretend you aren't."

Morgan stopped drawing.

In college, Amy had once gone to urgent care with a case of mono. It had been nothing major, but the nurses there had hooked her up to an I.V. to rehydrate her and get her through the worst of it.

When they'd flushed her line with cleaning saline in between the bags of fluids, Amy had felt cold run right through her veins.

That feeling had nothing on what she was feeling now.

Morgan hadn't busted out the bondage when they were having sex. There were no kinky works of art on the walls, or handcuffs in the bedroom.

There was only one place that Amy could have got that piece of information, and it was from somewhere that she wasn't supposed to have been.

And Morgan knew it.

From across the space between them, Morgan looked over at Amy. "What does that mean?"

"Uh," Amy's brain stuttered, like a skipping record, trying to find the right thing to say. "It's just the impression that I get, you know," she lied.

Neither of them had moved, but somehow the distance between them seemed to grow even greater. "Amy," Morgan said, low and slow, "did you go through my things?"

"I—look, I—it was a mistake!" she cried. "It was before I... we... look, I'm so sorry!"

Something in Morgan's expression crumpled inwards, like she'd been struck—and then the warm, loving person she'd just been talking to disappeared, and in her place was the implacable ice queen that Amy had first met in town.

"I should have known. I did know, actually, didn't I?" She let out a bark of completely humorless laughter. "This is my fault for changing my mind about you." Looking away from Amy, she turned on her heel.

"Morgan!" Amy stumbled from her seat towards the other woman. She needed to grab her, to tell her something, anything to make this right...

But there was nothing she could say. Don't take it personally—I was only invading your privacy for my job? She stumbled, her legs clumsy with pins and needles from sitting in the same position for so long. By the time she caught up with Morgan, she was in the mudroom, pulling on a jacket.

"When the bus comes, go." Morgan looped a scarf around her neck, her eyes focused on the door. On anywhere but Amy. "I won't see you again."

"Morgan, wait! I—"

Morgan didn't say anything else. What else was there to say, after all? She simply turned and left, slamming the door.

And that was that.

———— *ele* ————

Amy didn't know how long she cried. On the living room couch, the dogs surrounded her, tails wagging in confusion. Wet noses nuzzled at her, trying to help.

But her problems were a little more than could be helped by patting a cute dog.

She'd wanted a clear path to walk, hadn't she? Well, now she had it. All that Amy had to do now was walk onto the bus, and then let it carry her back to her home that she'd slaved for, and her job that she'd hunted down with every fiber of her drive, and that promotion that she'd been so thrilled to jump for.

Except...

Except that that home was empty, a bare little box that was just filled with the things that she'd thought she'd have to own to be A Real Professional.

Except that that job was something that she'd thought she'd desperately wanted... but somewhere along the line, it had turned her into someone willing to ditch their sense of human decency.

Except that that promotion came at the cost of forcing Morgan back into the spotlight against her will, just to line Savannah's pockets.

The option that her heart had wanted was gone. The option that her head had wanted was poisoned for her.

Shit.

Shit!

"I've ruined everything," Amy moaned. "What am I supposed to do—brr!"

An icy draught blew past, ruffling her hair. She shivered violently, and then looked up for the cause, blinking in confusion. The little cottage was usually toasty and warm—what the hell had that been?

She looked around her... and then froze.

When Morgan had stormed out, it had been through the front door, slamming it behind her.

The door that, with its warped frame, never closed easily.

The door that had been open the entire time.

Triple shit! Amy got to her feet, wiping clumsily at her tears with the heel of her hand. "Hey," she croaked between sniffles, "hey, dogs? Dogs? Roll call, little guys. Check, one, two, three."

There was Boris, and there was Muffin, and there were O.J. and Major, all wagging their tails in mild canine confusion but happy for the attention.

Amy sighed in relief. That was the whole of the familiar array of little faces, looking up at her like they had all week in hope of treats. Thank god.

The last thing she needed was to add insult to injury by losing one of Morgan's dogs in the snow—

No, wait. She'd made a mistake. Belatedly, her brain caught up to her and tugged urgently on her sleeve, trying to point something out.

All the little faces that she was used to seeing were here, sure. But not all of Morgan's pack were friendly, were they...?

Bella wasn't there.

Maybe she was just in another room. Of course she wouldn't come when Amy called—she didn't like people, after all. She was probably asleep on the couch, or under a bed, or whatever it was that loner dogs did when they weren't hanging around with the rest of their packs.

Amy raced through the rest of the cottage—the thoroughly Maltese-less cottage—then tugged the front door open again and looked out into the freshly-fallen snow.

There were a series of clear little dog paw prints leading off into the dark.

She looked up and down the street, but there was no Bella in sight. The trail of little prints rambled off around the bases of some nearby pine trees, and then...

...headed off into the woods.

Amy yanked on a jacket and a pair of gloves, and then grabbed a nearby flashlight and one of the leashes that was hanging on the mudroom hooks. The rest of the pack started to wag their tails and wiggle with excitement, but she desperately shushed them. "No no no, this isn't a walk, little guys! I need to find your sister."

How far could one small dog have got in the snow? Bella probably hadn't gone too far. She was so little, after all. Amy just needed to find her, and pick her up, and bring her home before her bus was due to leave.

She looked at the clock on the wall. She had an hour until her bus left.

The smart thing to do would have been to just leave, like she was scheduled to do—and just like Morgan wanted her to do. Dogs came home by themselves all the time, right? Where she'd grown up, people just let their dogs roam.

But the thought of walking out of Morgan's life while leaving her one dog down... just the idea of it made Amy want to puke from shame. She might have played the monster here, but she wasn't going to let herself be that much of a monster.

This wasn't in her planner. It was going to throw her plans, only just freshly back on track, into chaos.

But that didn't matter. Without a look back, Amy ran out of the door.

Chapter Twenty-One

Morgan

There were many good things about living in a small town, but it had its downsides, too.

A downside that Morgan had never previously appreciated about small places was this: when you went for a walk to cool off, you wound up doing laps. It made the whole affair feel ridiculous, which made her even more angry, which somehow only made her feel even more ridiculous.

You fool, she thought to herself, walking around the main block.

You were so cautious, but you wound up being played anyway, she thought, the second time around.

How much of it was real? How much of it was just Savannah sending Amy to mess with you?

Morgan crossed her arms more firmly, growling into her scarf. That probably wasn't the case. She was the wounded party, though. If she wanted to wallow in her own paranoia, she had every right to it.

At a glimpse of movement, Morgan looked to her side.

And accidentally locked eyes with Marie, who had been looking through the front window of the Bellbird, watching her march in circles for hours.

There was a pause as they stared at each other through the glass. Then, with a glower, Marie waved her in. With such a direct order, Morgan was unable to do anything but obey. She marched inside the Bellbird, wary of what was about to happen.

Marie gave her an appraising look, like a prize-fighter squaring up against their opponent. "It's cold out."

"Sure is."

"Coffee?"

"Thanks."

It was barely a conversation, but it was still more than Morgan was used to speaking with Marie. It was small progress, but it was still progress.

"Where's Amy?"

Morgan hunched her shoulders. "Gone—or about to be, anyway."

"You don't know?"

"I'm not the one driving the bus." Morgan hunkered further down, staring into her cup of coffee. "She was just staying in my guest room, after all. I'm not her keeper."

Marie tch'ed. "Really? She should have said something! I would have loved to see her off. I bet some of the others would have, too." She tutted. "Americans. What do they know about manners?"

Morgan raised an eyebrow. Marie held her gaze and looked back.

All right, Morgan thought, message received. Ouch.

"Still, though." Through her scowl, Marie looked a little puzzled. "I really thought she would have liked to say goodbye. She seemed like that sort of person."

"We... had a fight."

As soon as the line had left her lips, Morgan regretted it. It sounded so... juvenile.

Marie raised her eyebrows, but didn't comment. "Huh. I thought you two were getting along."

"She was just some reporter here to dig up dirt on me."

"Really." Marie gave Morgan an even look. "It didn't seem that way. Seemed like you liked her."

If the Bellbird ever went under, the woman would have had her path cut out for her in witness interrogation. Morgan felt vaguely like she should be asking for an attorney.

But... Marie wasn't wrong. Amy had swept into town, and she'd dragged Morgan out of her hiding hole—to the Lodge, to help Marie, to actually talk to her neighbors despite her urge to stay inside, licking her emotional wounds. It felt to Morgan like she must have spoken more words in the last week than she had in the whole of the last year.

And it had felt... good. Like opening a window on a stuffy room. Like taking off a cast.

"I did. I did like her." Morgan stared into her coffee.

And Amy had liked her back, too.

Amy had stuck her nose into Morgan's affairs, true... but she'd just been following her boss's orders. Everything that had happened past that point —that hadn't been an act. Now, removed from the heat of the moment, Morgan believed that. She dropped her head over her coffee, misery singeing hot and shameful through her.

Morgan had walked away from her career, but she'd had billions in her pocket. That didn't mean that anyone could just do that. What options did Amy have? Could Morgan blame Amy for doing her job?

"Marie to Planet Morgan." Marie's voice cut through Morgan's misery.

"Mmm?"

"Do you still know, like..." Marie gestured vaguely. "Famous people and things?"

Morgan had not been prepared for whatever line of questioning this was. "Yes? I haven't talked to anyone from my old life in a while, but there's a few people who'd still pick up the phone, I'd bet."

"Publishers and things like that?"

"Sure, some. I've given my fair share of forewords and promotional quotes in my time."

"Okay," Marie said, "here's the deal." She leaned forward and crossed her arms on the bar. "I'm going to give you some advice, and in exchange you're going to get in touch with some big fancy publishing people and get me an early copy of the next Reuben Reid book. I know they do that kind of thing."

Morgan stared back in open challenge. "I am?"

Marie met her gaze as coolly as any boardroom negotiator. "Yes, because no-one else is going to say it to you, and you need to hear it. Here's my advice, ready? Get the hell out of here, go back home, and apologize to her before she leaves."

Morgan looked back down. "You're making it sound like we're a couple."

Marie looked genuinely taken aback. "Aren't you?"

"What makes you think that?"

Marie gestured around her. "She got you out of the house. When you were out with her, you smiled. That was new."

"Maybe we were just friends."

Marie gave her a look. "You've got short hair."

"Jesus christ, that's not—" Morgan put her head in her hands. "Look, it doesn't matter. She's getting on the bus and leaving any moment now."

"So? Go apologize anyway. Look at you. You look even more miserable than usual. It can't get worse."

It can't get worse.

...That was true, wasn't it?

Even if this didn't work out, even if they didn't fall into each other's arms... Morgan didn't want this relationship to end the way her last one had: an argument, a sharp goodbye, and never looking back, with ruminating grudges and what-ifs running through her veins like poison for years.

She got to her feet, her head spinning. "I... I guess I will."

"Remember, the next book. Or else."

"Absolutely." Morgan let out a chuff of laughter. "Thanks, Marie."

"No worries. Go do your thing." Marie looked pointedly back down at Morgan's empty cup. "And the coffee will be five bucks."

Chapter Twenty-Two

Amy

Bella's paw-prints led up along the pine trees that lined the road. Amy followed along next to them, flashlight in hand, gritting her teeth and trying to remember every fact about following animal tracks that she'd ever picked up. The list wasn't long. Bear Grylls, you have failed me.

It looked like Bella had gone from tree to tree, sniffling and circling; for all of her hoity-toity nature, it seemed that she was just another dog after all. Then her path broke away, and it took Amy a moment to swing the flashlight around and find the track of paw prints in the snow.

Heading upwards into the mountain.

Goddamnit.

Amy jogged as best she could along the track, shining her flashlight on the paw prints. They were deep and clear to see in some places, where the snow was deep enough to be helpful, but shallower in other places, where Bella had walked across light snow and rock. It was getting harder and harder to keep sight of the little dog's track as it disappeared in one spot and reappeared in another seemingly out of nowhere.

Keep looking down, Ames, keep looking down...

There was a crack like a lightning strike, impossibly loud. Ahead of her, a tree bough fell to the ground in a crash, torn from the tree by the weight of the gathered snow weighing it down. Snow and pine needles sprayed everywhere, and then the world fell silent again.

Amy's heart beat in her chest. Um. Maybe look upwards once in a while, too.

Godamnit, New Zealand, I thought Australia was supposed to be the dangerous country!

Amy shuddered. Maybe this was a really dumb thing to do. Maybe she should just turn around now and go back down the mountain. It wasn't like she owned Morgan anything.

The thought turned her stomach.

She trudged on.

And then a few paces later, stopped. Something moved by the edge of the path, skulking alongside the prehistoric ferns. Something small, white, and furry.

"Bella!" For a moment, Amy could have kissed that damp little doggy nose. "Here, girl!"

Amy took a step forward. Bella took a couple of steps away, and then turned to keep Amy where she could see her, those dark eyes wary.

Shit. "C'mon, girl," Amy wheedled. "I know you don't like me, but it's cold. Don't you want to get back to your mom?"

She stepped closer... and Bella wheeled away and hurried off through the trees. At the dimmest edge of Amy's flashlight, Bella stopped and turned to look back at her, as far away as she could get without losing track of her pursuer.

Failure came in a lot of different shapes. Sometimes it was a big red F on a test. Sometimes it was a tight, bright smile and a "thanks, we'll call you," from an interviewer.

This was a new one, though: failure came in the form of a fluffy little Maltese, looking at her warily from a distance and refusing to come over.

One time, hours deep in a mindless Netflix binge, Amy had watched a documentary on deep sea exploration. She'd seen footage of a Coke can sinking to the bottom of the sea: the invisible pressure of the ocean had grown more and more intense, until suddenly it crumpled inwards, collapsing in on itself in a violent tangled wreck.

It wasn't the most poetic comparison, she knew. But at that moment, her and that Coke can? Siblings.

She laughed a giddy little laugh, and then she began to cry.

All of it hit her like a truck, and she opened herself up and let it rush through her.

Amy sat down heavily on the snow-covered ground, and wrapped her arms around her knees, and bawled, crying like she hadn't since she was a dumb little kid.

What good was she—to anyone? She'd thought she was some kind of hotshot, but all she was good for was being played by people. People like Savannah, and even her own self, just mindlessly following the schedule her past self had set down for her future self.

Stupid! She was just a stupid little pawn, too brainless to do anything but be pushed around and moved into place.

She was pathetic.

She was useless.

She was—ick, what the hell?

Something warm was on her face. Something warm, and wet, and upsettingly doggy.

Amy opened her eyes. Bella was standing next to her. With the most business-like body language Amy had ever seen on a dog, Bella leant up and licked her face again.

A memory rose up: she's good company when you need her, Morgan had said, days ago.

Amy hooked her fingers into Bella's collar and blubbered helplessly against the little dog's neck.

"You didn't put on your snow booties before you left," Amy babbled. Wiping away the tear-tracks that were starting to become decidedly chilly on her face, she reached out to Bella. Please let me do this...

Miracles did come true: without more than a weird look that clearly said we don't know each other well enough for this, but okay, Bella let Amy clip her leash on, and then wrap her arms around her and lift her up.

"For such a big problem, you sure don't weigh much," Amy managed with a hiccup. She hoisted Bella under her arm, and got back fully to her feet. "C'mon, little miss trouble, let's get you back to where it's warm and dry."

Here's what she was going to do, she thought to herself. She was going to follow her footsteps back to town, and she was going to hand Bella over to the first person she saw, because if she saw Morgan again she was going to crumple up and cry piteously. She'd had a long day, okay, and she had approximately zero percent inner fortitude left, and there was no way she was getting out of seeing Morgan again with her dignity intact and her head held high.

Amy turned, and then froze.

She'd been running back and forth through the forest.

Her footprints were all over the place.

She ran her eyes back and forth over the mess. Had she come from... over there, maybe? She trudged over, following one set of prints, but then a few moments later, frowned as the trail began to lead upward. Okay, no, this was a dead end. After she came this way, she... turned around... and then went left? Or right?

Sometimes the most horrible moments in your life came with loud noises and fanfare, like a car crash or someone screaming in your face. Sometimes, though, the worst moments came with a strange silence.

In the muffled quiet of the night, Amy stood and watched as the falling snow began to fill her footprints in. In her arms, Bella shivered.

Okay, time for a plan.

Amy had no plan.

Um. Okay. Time for the sort of plan you made when you had no plan?

What were you supposed to do at that point, again?

Somewhere off in the darkness surrounding them, another tree branch crashed to the ground.

"I really should have watched more Bear Grylls," Amy said to Bella, who didn't dignify that with a response.

Chapter Twenty-Three

Morgan

Morgan stood in front of her front door, and took a deep breath. Marie had been right. She was also a cold-blooded cut-throat mercenary, charging five dollars for a cup of coffee—but she was right. Morgan needed to end this on better terms. She'd already once tried walking away from broken-hearted love with her heart full of unsaid things. It hadn't worked out particularly well for her.

She opened the front door of the cottage, and found an empty house.

It was exactly what she'd wanted, an hour ago. It was precisely what she'd asked for.

It didn't feel like a victory.

She absent-mindedly stroked the dogs' heads as she walked through her house, operating on autopilot. It had been her home for three years— but now, silent save for the sound of paws and her own footsteps, it felt alien to her.

She sighed when she passed the guest room door. Tch, a guest room. What a stupid idea. Who had she been expecting to stay? With her?

"Amy?"

The house was quiet. Morgan checked her watch, just in case. There was still time before the bus came.

Amy must have left early.

Morgan exhaled. Well. Okay. New plan: she needed to turn around and head over to the visitor's center—

She froze.

Through the half-open door, she could see Amy's things still on the bed.

Cautiously, Morgan pushed the door open. "Amy?"

There was no response. She hadn't expected one—by now, Amy should have been at the visitor's center, waiting for the transfer bus to take her on her way back to Auckland, irrevocably on a trajectory out of Morgan's life. Gone for good. Exactly the way that Morgan had demanded.

And, okay, maybe it was obvious that Amy might leave some things behind. They hadn't exactly parted on good terms. Morgan chewed her lower lip as the memory of Amy's face haunted her—those big dark eyes wide with something like horror, trying to hide the way that her hands were trembling.

So maybe it just made sense that she'd left behind some things as she'd got ready to leave, whether by accident or just because she couldn't be bothered taking them with her. Morgan's mouth twisted to the side as she picked up one of the souvenir sweaters that Amy had been forced to wear. Lord knows that if Morgan was fleeing a scene like that, she wouldn't exactly be dying to hang on to a violently purple jumper with a picture of a dancing beet emblazoned on the front.

But underneath the sweater, left on the bed, was Amy's phone.

"Amy? Are you still here?" she repeated, but the house was still quiet. Her brow furrowed, Morgan stalked through her house.

There was no sign of Amy, or a note saying—what? Morgan wasn't sure what sort of thing to be expecting. As she looked through the rest of the house for a clue, she could almost hear Amy's voice in her head, saying something ridiculous like I'm leaving it all behind to become a Buddhist monk, please donate all my earthly possessions to orphans, or kittens, or orphaned kittens.

But there was nothing.

Something had gone wrong.

Morgan turned back to the doorway, and grabbed her jacket back from the hook by the door.

ele

Within minutes, she was over at the Red Deer Lodge. The place was busy, locals making the best of the snowy weather outside by drinking and eating, laughing and chatting.

Just one scant week ago, the idea of interrupting the crowd of people, all busy with their warm little lives and certainly not interested in her problems, would have made Morgan want to sink into the floor.

Now, though, it didn't cross her mind.

Without pausing, she stuck her fingers into her mouth, and whistled. Heads turned to her.

"Has anyone seen Amy—that American reporter—this evening?"

There was the general hubbub of a mass of people checking with each other, hemming and hawing with the American? Did I see her over at—no, that was yesterday—wasn't she supposed to leave—then general shrugs and shakes of the head.

"No dice?" said James, behind the bar. "Why, what's up?"

"She's missing."

"Are you sure?"

A week ago, with so many eyes on her, Morgan might have crumbled under the attention.

Amy was a grown woman. How could Morgan be sure that something was wrong? They'd had a fight—maybe Amy had just walked out on her. Maybe Morgan was just causing a fuss for no reason. Everyone would gossip about that one for ages: the weirdo who called in the cavalry because her kind-of-sort-of fling stormed off one time...

Now, though, she was certain.

There was a problem.

And she needed to fix it.

As people started getting to their feet, Morgan drew her shoulders back, standing tall. "You, you, you: come with me, to the east. I need some people to sweep west—good, thank you. Who has the keys to the town emergency gear? Great, we'll need flashlights and walkie-talkies. Meet us out there."

She turned on her heel, ready to get into action, and the townspeople rallied behind her.

Chapter Twenty-Four

Amy

Okay, the forests of New Zealand were truly as beautiful and majestic as all the tourism copywriting had promised.

However, one thing that the brochures sure hadn't covered was the fact that they were also a labyrinth from hell.

Okay, Ames, you can do this, she thought, trudging through the snowy forest with Bella in her arms. You were not put on this planet to freeze to death half an hour away from civilization. That's a just plain embarrassing way to die. And if you're happy to die in an embarrassing way, then get out of here first, and workshop a better scene later. Preferably something with a dozen hot women and a sex act gone wrong.

She took a breath and looked around her. Nothing jumped out at her, not a single clue helpfully letting her know if she was walking towards the town or further away from it into the forest.

Thinking hard, she looked up.

The trees that surrounded her were huge, but even they couldn't block out the sky entirely. Holding Bella close, Amy craned her head up to look upwards.

Above her were the stars.

The same stars that had been above her when she'd been in Morgan's al fresco bath.

Well, the first time, anyway, not the second time. Though she certainly had seen stars that time, too.

She frowned, thinking. Okay, she wasn't exactly astronomer material—she never even managed to remember what her moon sign was—but she could remember some things.

From Morgan's cottage, she had followed Bella into the woods to the left. When she'd been in the bath, a really bright set of stars had been visible on the right.

She could see the same set of stars now, waiting on the horizon. So if she went towards that constellation... that would take her toward the town, right?

That made total sense. On the other hand, she'd also seen a documentary one time that said that when people were freezing to death, their brains also started malfunctioning, telling them things like the best thing to do in the moment was to take off all their clothes and run around naked in the snow.

This didn't feel like a malfunction. It felt like a sensible thing to do. Right?

"Don't let me get naked," she commanded Bella as she started walking towards the stars. "If I start acting out the world's weirdest version of Girls Gone Wild, you have full permission to bite me. You got that?"

Bella wagged her tail.

"I'll take that as a yes," Amy said, and sloughed off through the snow.

Amy followed her stars, sometimes losing them behind the trees, then re-emerging into a clearing to find them again.

They didn't seem to be getting any closer, but they didn't seem to be getting any further, either.

"Is this the way home, girl?" she asked her furry passenger, but only got a bored sigh in response.

"You're the worst Wilson ever," she grumbled, her teeth chattering. But despite her unhelpfulness, Bella's warm weight, snuggling against her chest, kept her grounded.

Amy needed to do this.

She needed to bring Bella home.

Something flashed, lower than the constellation. Down in the trees.

A flashlight!

The ray of light cut through the trees, searching. "Amy?"

Amy's knees trembled, threatening to give out. "Morgan? Morgan!"

She stumbled forward, squinting, slip-sliding down a snow-covered incline. In her arms, Bella wiggled eagerly, ears pricked up for her master's voice.

They crashed into each other's' arms. Morgan ran her hands over Amy, checking her for injuries, and then came back up to hold her face in her hands. "Amy, I'm so—Are you okay?"

The urge to cry rose back up in Amy's chest, unbearable. She shoved Bella out from her, holding her out to Morgan. "Bella—Bella—"

"What's wrong with her?"

"M-make sure she's okay, too."

Morgan looked her over quickly, skating her fingers over Bella's face and then down to squeeze her paws. The little Maltese wriggled unhappily in Amy's grasp, clearly well and truly over her quota of social interaction for the day. "What's wrong with her?" Morgan asked, alarmed. "She looks fine."

"Oh, good," Amy said with a giddy little smile, and then she burst into tears.

"Oh, Amy," Morgan started, and then she drew her into her arms.

"I know I did something terrible—" Amy sobbed, "but I don't want to be that much of a monster. I don't want to be that person."

Morgan tucked Amy against her, cradling her close. "Let's get you home."

It didn't take long. Morgan called to the rest of the townspeople, and Amy let Morgan draw her through the loose crowd, offering she's okays and other things over Amy's head as she focused on putting one foot in front of the other, Bella trotting right next to her legs.

When they got to the cottage, Amy hesitated at the front step, unwilling and unsure. "Morgan, I—"

"No talk." Without another word, Morgan gently but firmly marched her back inside. She deposited the perfectly fine Bella in the living room, the fireplace stoked high, and left her to the investigation of the other dogs, sniffing her from her nose to the tip of her tail, curious about her strange expedition.

That done, Morgan marched Amy through to the bathroom, and then, without any further warning, began to strip her from her snow-soaked clothes.

"W-woah, Morgan," Amy managed with wide eyes and chattering teeth. "I-I'm flattered, b-but I'm not sure—"

"Not for that." Morgan rolled her eyes. "You're cold. Get in the shower."

Amy shuddered as she was frog-marched into the shower; the warm water stung her frozen extremities, biting at her nose and fingers.

"All fingers and toes accounted for?"

Amy let out a thin laugh. "People talk about leaving their hearts in other countries, but it's not so poetic to leave your toes behind." She wiggled her toes compliantly. "All here. I'm fine. I'm just cold."

They looked at each other. There was an uncertainty on Morgan's face, something sad... but longing.

Amy had strode through the snow towards her guiding stars.

Now, she wasn't going to stay adrift just out of fear. Somewhere along the line, in the face of her regrets and her fear, all of that had started to seem unimportant. "Let's talk," she said.

"Was sleeping with me all part of your plan?"

Amy slumped back against the tiled shower wall, fighting the urge to curl in on herself. "No. Savannah hoped that me being your type would get me far—but I didn't know about that until after."

Morgan made a face like she'd bit into a lemon. "Trust her to think that I'd still be into someone who reminded me of her, even after what she did."

Amy declined to comment on that particular point. "I didn't know anything until I was here and starting to put things together, and then she asked me to snoop..."

She dropped her eyes to the ground. "I figured it out too late. That meant I played right into her hand. She knew that outright asking me to sleep with you was a bridge too far. But if I was already here, and I just happened to get you to fall for me, well... that's something else entirely. After that, then she could pressure me into writing about it." She looked up. "I'm not going to, by the way."

Morgan sighed. "I... I know that, now."

"But if I don't write the article that she wants, then I lose my career. My apartment. Everything that makes up my life."

"I'm not going to say that stepping away from your life is an easy thing to do." Morgan's mouth quirked ruefully to the side. "I only did it because I was running away from everything. If you hadn't come to town, I would have stayed that way—always running away."

Exhaling deeply, Amy turned off the shower. Morgan took her hand as she stepped out of it, slinging a big, fluffy towel around her. Amy wrapped herself in it, and then looked up at Morgan. "You know what? I think I'm okay with losing everything. If that life was shaping me into the kind of person who'd do that... then it's not a good one. It might have been fancier than where I grew up, but it was just trading one trap for another." She sighed. "Even if I'll miss my apartment."

Morgan looked down at her. "What are you going to do now?"

Amy laughed. Something fierce bubbled up in her, her vision now clear.

Maybe it was the effects of a near-death experience. Maybe it was hypothermia. Whatever it was, it felt good.

"I'm going to quit," Amy said, decisive. "And then..."

"And then?"

Amy turned to look up at Morgan with a smile that was wrung-out but happy. "I don't know. I don't know what to do next!" she said, for the first time in her life.

She nestled in against Morgan. "But... I'll find it out as I go."

Morgan held her close. "I still have money, you know. I could—"

"No." Clasped together, Amy's hand tightened on Morgan's. "I don't want to rely on what you could give me. I got myself out of a bad situation once..." She took a breath. "I was so focused on not going backward, that I lost track of what that really means. If I got myself out of a bad place once, that just means that I can do it again."

She made a face. "Even if it means a few years of doing gig work and then coming home to bang out endless Which 80s Cartoon's Annoying Talking Animal Sidekick Are You? quizzes."

Morgan pressed a kiss to her forehead. "Just don't make me Scrappy Doo."

Amy laughed. "And... what about you?" She dropped her eyes, focusing on the sight of Morgan's fingers intertwined with her own. "I know you never wanted to come out to the world. If I quit, it'll piss Savannah off something fierce. She might just spill her guts to spite you."

"You know that everyone in town thinks that we're together, anyway, right?"

"They do?"

Morgan nodded. "Which made me feel like a real fool, I can tell you that." She pulled Amy closer, running her fingers through Amy's damp locks, tucking them out of her face. "Have you ever worried about something—finding a strange new bump, say—for months, running through every disaster scenario in your mind... and then when you finally gather the bravery to get it checked out, it turns out to be nothing?"

"Oh man, do I ever."

Morgan smiled wryly. "It was something like that."

"I'm your weird bump? Morgan Leithe, you're such a romantic."

She nudged Morgan's shoulder with her own; Morgan did it right back. "So," Morgan said, clearly not willing to be distracted from the important things. "I think... I think that I'm fine with where I am. With people knowing who I am." She looked up. "But what are you going to say to Savannah now?"

"That's the million dollar question, isn't it? Now that I've given everything up..." Amy squared her shoulders. "I have some thoughts in mind."

Chapter Twenty-Five

Georgie

If the kid behind her didn't stop kicking her seat, Georgie was going to throw him out the nearest emergency exit.

It would be a headline news story: reporter snaps, plane grounded, kid with world's pointiest feet mourned by no-one. She'd write it herself, in handcuffs, down in her cell and all.

In the middle of daydreaming about the photo of her that would run next to the story—she'd have to fix her eyeliner before she was arrested, of course—the person next to her, snoring, slid down in his seat a little and jammed his elbow into her ribs.

Again.

Grimacing, Georgie used her phone to push his elbow back over the demilitarized zone of the arm rest.

The journalism industry was cutthroat—but she had never before wanted to take that quite so literally.

She let out a sigh, and slithered down in her chair as far as the seatbelt would allow her.

Sure, she'd got her big story, all the Ts dotted and all the Is crossed—or whatever. Sure, Savannah had praised her work... but then she'd refused to make a judgment on who got the promotion, stringing Georgie along with a smile until Amy's work was in to compare against. She wanted Georgie to be threatened.

Savannah may have had dear sweet little farm girl Amy dancing to her tune, but Georgie was so over it. She'd been rubbing elbows with CEOs ever since she was young enough to say trust fund.

Savannah was coming across as desperate.

Georgie did not like desperate people. Ugh.

Her phone buzzed, distracting her from her thoughts. She looked down at a text from Amy.

Nice trip?

Omg, the best!! she typed back.

Georgie shoved aside her snoring flightmate and angled herself so that her camera caught nothing but her and the view outside of the window, cutting off the rest. She artfully posed her face, snapped a photo of her best angle, made some quick adjustments to erase the dark smudges under her eyes, and then sent it. Feeling refreshed, radiant, and blessed!

So, are you happy with your article?

Yep. It's great. This promotion is mine, babe.

True! Because I'm quitting. :) The field's all clear for you.

Georgie forcefully shoved the elbow out of her side again and stared at her phone. What the hell? Tell me more.

I can do more than tell you, Amy replied. Do you want to help out?

_el_

By the end of the flight, Georgie's head was spinning. All thoughts of rude children and cramped seats had been wiped away, replaced with scheming and plotting.

That was a definite improvement in her books.

In the taxi back to her apartment, she opened up her serious contact list.

Is anyone working on anything adjacent to blackmail in journalism right now? she posted. I have a source to pass on. Serious stuff.

As the replies started to come in, she opened up her Whatsapp group.

Soooo who wants some spicy blind items? I have some insider goss. Serious stuff!

Chapter Twenty-Six

Savannah

This whole affair with Leithe was a royal pain in the ass.

Most things in journalism were pains in the asses, Savannah had come to learn. When she'd first—ahem—acquired her seed money, she'd been in love with the idea of being a CEO at a media company. Flying around the world to interview celebs, having all the hot new up-and-comers knocking on her door, begging for the exposure that she could give them... and, more importantly, hiring people to do the bulk of the work for her.

It had all sounded good on paper. But you know what hadn't sounded good? The constant news of media companies going bust. No, Savannah had sworn, she wasn't going to wind up the same way.

So one quick bit of unpleasant contact later, she'd had the tech world's most longed-for interview on the hook—and if her hot little understudy reporter could just do her thing and turn on the charm like she always did, there was a chance at something a little more exciting.

The snowstorm had been a bonus. The increasing resistance she'd felt from Amy through her emails, though, had not.

And now, radio silence.

Savannah glared at her phone as she refreshed her inbox. Amy's flight had left nearly twenty hours ago. She should be well and truly back home, bags collected, taxi flagged, apartment returned to. There was no excuse for going incommunicado. She wasn't in the backwoods of some bumpkin country any more.

She tossed her phone back on to her desk with a scowl. Even if Amy did bring her the goods, she'd decided, she'd be giving the lead reporter position to Georgie. Georgie had already reported back from her travel, slightly more tanned, some solid writing and tantalizing new leads in hand. She'd immediately thrown herself back into her work without fuss, sitting back at her desk, wildly typing away on some new project like a good little reporter should. Georgie wasn't ignoring her boss, that was for sure.

Her email alert chimed. Finally! With a sigh of happiness, Savannah reached for her phone.

Before she could even pick it up, it chimed again.

And again.

And again?

Savannah squinted at her rapidly-chiming phone like it had sprouted beetle legs and begun to crawl across her desk. Cautiously, she picked it up and unlocked it.

omg Savannah did you really??? asked a friend.

what did you do? please tell me what's happening! said another.

Another, far less concerned text simply read Due to recent allegations, we will not be continuing our advertisement agreement schedule with Zero Nova.

Savannah opened her email, and began to read.

According to what people were asking her to confirm or deny, she'd had a secret relationship with a public figure, and blackmailed them into funding her company.

But the list of public figures was long. It seemed that every single message about it had a completely different person in mind:

sooo I heard you homewrecked the guy from VirtualTech lmao

Hun did you really seduce that guy from google

omg savvie, that ted talk guy??? he's like a billion years old

Savannah threw open her door and stormed down the hallway into the main office.

The main office... that was now a little emptier than it had been that morning.

On the bare desk that used to be Georgie's were two things: an itemized report for travel expenses, and her resignation letter.

That bitch! Seething, Savannah opened the highest-profile contact in her phone and hit call. The Herald was a big-ticket newspaper, and its CEO owed her a favor.

If Amy—and Georgie, too, because apparently disloyalty was contagious —wanted to try to cover up Savannah's relationship with Morgan by burying it in lies, then Savannah was just going to flip their script and tell the truth.

"Good morning, this is John Rowling-Smith's office, how can I help you?"

"This is Savannah Whitney. Put me through to John, I have a story for him."

"I'm sorry, ma'am," the receptionist said. "John is busy at the moment. I'll put you through to the writer's room, one moment."

"What? No, I don't want to talk to some writer, I want to talk to—"

"Hello, Matias speaking."

Savannah fumed. "This is Savannah at Zero Nova. I want an exposé written on my secret affair with Morgan Leithe. I have full details to provide."

"Ah. I see." There was a pause, and then... was he trying to hold back a laugh?

"Is there something funny about that?" Savannah snarled.

"Oh, no, I'm sorry," the man she was speaking to corrected himself. "It's just..."

"It's just what?"

"Well, that would be... hmm, it's not the least likely person I've heard rumors about those blind items being on, but it's pretty damn close. I don't think we can run that, ma'am. Everyone's money is on it being a certain TED Talk speaker, or the head of VirtualTech. Do you happen to have any details about them, instead?"

"What the fuck are you talking about, you wretched little man?"

"It being Leithe..." He made an unimpressed sound. "That just sounds desperate. It's too far-fetched. I don't think our readers will buy that, when they have so many other, better options to believe."

Her phone pressed to her ear, Savannah stared blankly into space. "But it's true!"

"Leithe? Come on, ma'am."

In the midst of her horror, Savannah became aware of something. "You sound familiar. Do I know you?"

"You have a nice day, ma'am," said Matias, ex-Zero Nova writer. Hanging up, he happily went back to his new job, where he was allowed as many plants on his desk as he wanted.

✑ ✑ ✑

"You're playing with fire."

"Sure, I know that." When Savannah had calmed down from her DEFCON-1 shrieking fit and called the most likely suspect, she had expected Amy to sound either smug and satisfied, or scared and scurrying. Instead, she just sounded... normal, like she was having a perfectly average conversation with an acquaintance.

"You know what this means." Savannah ticked down items on her fingers. "No job means no income. No me in your corner means no career. No apartment means no life in New York. No income, no job, and no place to live means that you'll have to go crawling back home."

"There's a few problems with what you've just said, there. I might be fired—"

"Oh, you're so fired."

"—but I'll find another job. Even if you do try to badmouth me over there."

Over there? There was the sound of things moving in the background of Amy's call... and was that a bark? Savannah frowned. "Where are you? You're supposed to be back in NY."

"Um, yeah, about that. There was an incident with a dog—long story short, I missed the flight. I'm still in New Zealand."

"Oh." Something clicked into place. Savannah sat back in her chair, smug. "Oh. I see. You're Morgan's new sugar baby, huh? You got out of the rat race just to become someone's pet."

Instead of trying to defend it, Amy... laughed? "Nope! Savannah, you really have to stop thinking that everyone thinks the same way that you do." She swapped her phone to her other ear. "I realized that something that gets built up the wrong way is going to keep taking you the wrong way. I'm starting from scratch."

"You're giving up."

"I'm starting over," Amy repeated, with a smile in her voice. "And, you know, there's nothing wrong with that. Now, if you'll excuse me, I have a ball to throw."

And, just like that, Amy hung up.

On the other side of the world, Amy let out a deep breath. It had taken all of her strength to keep her voice steady. Savannah didn't need to know that her hands had been shaking the entire time.

"This is crazy," she said. "I don't know what to do with myself."

"I know," Morgan agreed. "But I have faith that you can figure something out."

"You know what?" Amy said, tucking her hand into Morgan's. "For once, I think I do, too."

Running ahead of them as they walked through the snow, the pack of dogs romped and rambled, chasing after a tennis ball.

And, down by Morgan and Amy's feet, Bella trotted along with them, keeping a haughty eye on the rest of her boisterous siblings.

Not too close, of course.

But close enough.

Chapter Twenty-Seven

Amy

"It says on your CV that your last position was with Zero Nova Media, over in the States?"

Amy nodded. "I apologize for not having a reference—the company folded after I left, and the boss is out of touch."

"Oh, I read about that," the interviewer said. "Nasty business."

And on that matter, that was that.

Savannah had been a medium fish in a big pond—but there were other ponds, puddles, and paddling pools in the world, if you were ready to go look for them.

Here, on the other side of the world, Amy smiled, free.

"We've read some of the work you did for Zero Nova, though. Good stuff." He looked across the table from her. Behind him were stylish art deco posters of planetary orbits, with depictions of microsatellites spinning around a globe below. "Now, do you know anything about space?"

"I know about consumer and business technologies," Amy said, with a twinkle in her eye. "And really, what's a satellite other than a really, really fancy phone?"

~ele~

Amy stowed her bag under her seat, double-checking that it was there (I'm never going through that again!). As the scenery outside the bus windows changed from city streets to emerald-green hills, and beautiful farmland scenery stretched out around her, she smiled to herself and started going over her notes.

There were a lot of things to consider, facts and figures and locations, timeframes to consider and documents to sign. She pored over it all, frowning slightly as she took it all in, and automatically put her hand into her purse.

She pulled out her planner. It was this year's new edition, the blank pages fresh and waiting to be filled with plans and preparations—but then, she paused. Her fingers traced over the days and weeks and months ahead of her, waiting to be filled.

Amy made a decision.

———ell———

When Amy stepped off the bus eight hours later, it was into a picture-perfect scene. A small, babbling creek; small, chirping birds in the undergrowth; the smell of wood smoke in the air.

It was perfect.

Okay, there was still no hot yoga, and the wifi was still terrible—but, she decided, she could cope with that.

Despite the bag on her back, it wasn't a long walk to where she wanted to go.

Even before she turned the corner to Morgan's cottage, she heard voices.

"That twist was fine!"

"It was not fine! Since when can fae breed with werewolves? Since when can someone be a werefae?!"

Amy laughed to herself. Marie was on the veranda with Morgan, both of them clearly in the middle of a heated argument. They were both holding copies of the new book, both books bristling with enough post-it notes and bookmarks to put a law student's textbooks to shame.

By their feet, the dogs lolled, unconcerned by the debate. Major and Boris had their oversized, blocky heads in Marie's lap, their eyebrows rising as they looked up from time to time in hopes that she'd stop angrily flipping through pages and go back to patting them. O.J. and Muffin were squashed up together in the armchair, Muffin looking rather uncomfortably pressed underneath the heavy weight of O.J., but clearly too lazy to move. Bella sat close enough to watch the circus unfold: high praise from the stand-offish little dog.

"Oh, hullo again, Amy!" Marie said, when she noticed that they weren't alone. "You in town for long this time?"

"Just the weekend again," Amy replied. "Auckland's keeping me busy."

"I'll leave you two to it, then," Marie said, getting to her feet. "Besides, if I hear any more defenses of bad plot twists again, I'm going to go crazy."

"Ryghlee being secretly a werefae was genius," Morgan declared. "The hints were there all along, if you knew where to look."

"Pfah!" Marie waved a hand dismissively in the air, and then dispensed pats to the dogs. "Bye, boys, girls. Your mother has terrible taste."

Amy laughed as Marie made her escape, and then she put her bag down, rolling her bus-stiff shoulders with a wince.

"Stiff?"

"No sane human designed long-distance bus seats," she declared, then shot Morgan a wicked smile. "Make it better?"

Morgan opened her arms, and Amy fell forward into them with a sigh.

No matter how long it had actually been since she saw Morgan last, coming home always felt like it had been a hundred years.

"How was it?" Morgan asked against her hair.

"I got the job," she said. "I start next week."

"Amy, that's great news!"

"It is! It means I'll be busy—really busy. But I can come over here on the weekends."

"I can go over there during the week, too."

Amy pulled back and looked up at her. "You'd do that? You'd head into the big city?"

Morgan shrugged a shoulder. "It's about time I did some proper sightseeing, isn't it? If people see me... well, then they see me."

"Is that.... is that okay?" Amy held her gaze. "I know you like your life quiet and predictable, and I don't like having someone all up in my business 24/7, either..." Her eyes sparkled. "But maybe we can find a way to not drive each other crazy."

"I think we can work something out," Morgan said, with a laugh. "Now, get inside. The fire's roaring."

Together, they went inside into the warm, cozy cottage.

Into Morgan's home.

And now, in part, Amy's too.

elle

Amy had built herself up from nothing before. If her new career fell apart, if this new, tentative happiness wasn't made to last—well, then she'd put on her big girl pants and climb that mountain again. Maybe it'd be harder that time, and maybe it'd take longer, but she'd make it in the end.

Until then, though, she could let herself enjoy her life as it came.

When the bus finished refueling and pulled back out of town, the unused planner was still on Amy's seat.

She didn't need it any more.

Thank you for reading A Dog Named Bella! Join the community of lesfic readers — share your thoughts about this story on Amazon or Goodreads.

ABOUT THE AUTHOR

Bel Blackwood spins stories of flawed women finding happiness, aimed at readers who like their lesbian romances to be heartfelt, quirky, and funny.

When she's not writing, Bel loves hiking with her mutts, baking up a storm, and trying (and failing) to learn to meditate. If she followed the advice to write what you know, all of her books would be about heroines waging war on the caterpillars eating their zucchini plants.

She isn't on social media, but can be found at her newsletter, where she spills the beans on new releases and upcoming books.

ALSO BY BEL BLACKWOOD

A Dog Named Bella (Small Town Sparks #1)
Smoke and Sugar (Small Town Sparks #2)
Free Flight (Small Town Sparks #3)
Always Hers

SMOKE AND SUGAR

<u>You can never plan for love. You definitely can't plan for llamas.</u>

Practical, down-to-earth Kaia Kingsley loves life in the rural wilds of New Zealand. Even if country life comes with its own challenges: keeping the bank from repossessing her farm, keeping her jam-making business afloat, and... finding a llama in her strawberry patch?

When she drags it back home, she doesn't expect its owner to be a gorgeous older woman. Tessa is icy, but Kaia can see the lonely woman under the surface... and she wants to see more.

But when Kingsley Jams gets the chance to enter in a famous food competition, Kaia needs to focus. If she doesn't win, her jam business will go under, taking her farm with it.

But the only person who can help her win is the biggest distraction of them all.

Her jams are made to make a person crave more. But now, Kaia is the one wrestling with sweet temptation.

<u>She went searching for a new life. She found new love.</u>

It's been six months since high-powered lawyer Tessa's breakup, but her ex's words are still ringing in her ears: Tessa Wright, you're heartless.

A small New Zealand town is the perfect place for Tessa to lick her wounds. But life in the country comes with challenges she wasn't prepared for—like her new neighbor, Kaia.

The younger woman is as sweet as the jam she makes. Tessa needs to stay away from her. Kaia deserves better than a cold-hearted city lawyer.

But when Kaia begs for her help saving her business, Tessa can't say no. As the competition day approaches, the two of them will have to work together. To save what Kaia holds dear, Tessa will have to learn to listen to her heart.

Smoke and Sugar is the second book in the Small Town Sparks series, but can be read as a standalone novel.

Printed in Great Britain
by Amazon